I0784863

TRACY SCHULDT HELIXON

The Book of Roisins

Tracy Schuldt Helixon

Copyright © 2025 by Tracy Schuldt Helixon
Published by Aisling Books, an imprint of Winged Publications

Editor: Cynthia Hickey
Book Design by Winged Publications

All rights reserved. No part of this publication may be reproduced, stored in a retrieval system, or transmitted in any form or by any means—electronic, mechanical, photocopying, recording, or otherwise—without the prior written permission of the publisher. The only exception is brief quotations in printed reviews. Piracy is illegal. Thank you for respecting the hard work of this author.

This book is a work of fiction. Names, characters, Places, incidents, and dialogues are either products of the author's imagination or used fictitiously.

Any resemblance to actual persons, living or dead, or events is coincidental.

ISBN: 978-1-965352-96-0

Dedication: To Tess and Jan, my daughter Ellie, my sisters Julie, Jessie, Mira, Linda, Lora, and Jenny, and all the women in our Schuldt, Walker, and Helixon sisterhood. You are my real-life Roisins.

.

Chapter One:

The Scrapbook

Present Day

I stare at my reflection and tug my left pigtail to make it even with the right. *Nope.* Not even close. It's almost time to go, though, so I give up on my hair and just start practicing. I look in the mirror and smile.

"Hi! I'm Roisin."

Too peppy. Cut the smile.

"Hello. My name is Roisin."

Too formal. Try something shorter.

"Roisin here."

What am I, a news reporter?

Ugh! It's no use. No matter how many times I

try, the words never come out right in front of a new class. And I should know. Four different schools by the middle of sixth grade. Not that I'm counting or anything.

Mom calls from downstairs. "Come on, Roisin! Don't be late on your first day."

I smell bacon and pancakes on my walk to the kitchen. Gran always cooks something special on the first day at a new school.

Dad has already left for his new job at Fort McCoy, but Mom's standing at the counter drinking coffee. My four brothers–Connor, Patrick, Joe, and Aidan–are sitting at the table with Gran. The plate in the middle has one piece of bacon left.

I reach for it, but Joe intercepts. "Snoozer-loser," he chimes, shoving the bacon in his mouth.

Gran takes the bacon from her plate and sets it on mine. "Here you go, honey," she says. "I couldn't eat another bite."

I glare at Joe, then muster a half smile for Gran. "Thanks," I tell her. Gran always looks out for me.

After a quick breakfast, I grab my backpack and head for the door.

"Ádh mór ort," says Mom.

"Yes – ádh mór ort, Miss Roisin!" adds Gran. The phrase means "good luck" in Irish Gaelic, and Mom and Gran always say it before a big event.

I thank them. Usually, I secretly hate that phrase—and all the Irish stuff along with it. Being new is bad enough without a face full of freckles, a head full of frizzy red curls, and an old, outdated name going back way too far.

Today, though, I'll accept the good luck wish, no matter what language it comes in. Something tells me I'm going to need it.

~~~~~

"Name, please?"

My heart thumps so hard I can feel it in my ears. As school offices go—and trust me, I've seen my share—this one has lots of space. So why does it suddenly feel like the time when Mom took us on the subway in New York City? After the Army transferred us there, Mom said it was time to explore how to get around in our new home. She called it an adventure. I called it being trapped in a scary underground tunnel with no end in sight.

New town, same story. *Scary and trapped.* The pancakes Gran made this morning are churning in my stomach.

The lady clears her throat and asks a second time, just a little louder. "Your name?"

I mean, it's not a hard question, but I still don't want to answer it. A bunch of alternatives run through my mind. Popular girls from my last three schools. *Bella. Sophia. Zoey. Ashley.* No one here knows me yet. Couldn't I just—reinvent myself?
~~~~~

The lady's forehead wrinkles. "Are you all right, dear?"

I catch my reflection in the tinted window behind her. Who am I kidding? Even if I could change my name, these frizzy red curls and freckles aren't going anywhere.

"Sorry," I say. "I'm new here. My mom registered me last week."

Her eyes brighten. "Oh! Of course. We've been expecting you." She opens a folder on the desk. "Welcome—"

And, there it is.

The pause.

"Royzin? Royzin Schwartz?"

I mean, to be fair, if I didn't know better, I would think *Roisin* is pronounced like *raisin,* too. I give her the smile I always give when someone mispronounces my name. She can't help it, and there's no use in both of us feeling miserable.

"Row-sheen," I tell her. "Like what you do in a boat, and then *sheen.* "

"Row-sheen," she says back slowly. "What a lovely name."

*Right, "lovely." * I just nod.

The Schwartz comes from my dad. He's in the Army, which is why I'm currently standing in a new school in Middle-of-Nowhere, Wisconsin. The Roisin comes from my mom. And my grandma. And lots of grandmas before that. My brothers got normal names. I got *Roisin.*

"You'll be in Mr. Garcia's room, number 127." She points to her left. "It's on the first floor, near the end of the hallway." She turns to check the time on the round white clock behind her. Every school office I've ever been in has one of those clocks. It's like it's a requirement or something. "Recess will be ending in just a few minutes. You can either go outside, or head to your classroom a little early to get settled." She hands me a piece of paper with my name and some other random details on it. "Please give this to your teacher when you get there."

Being new never gets easier. Maybe this time, I won't even try to fit in.

I grip the paper and head out the office door. My feet feel heavy, like somebody just poured bags of sand in my shoes. Let's see. Option One—Find my classroom early. Option Two—Go to the playground. Listen to my stomach growl as it ties itself in knots. Stand there. Avoid eye contact. Try to act like I belong. You know, like I'm just waiting for my three besties to meet up in our regular spot so we can hang out and stuff.

I suck in a breath. Option one it is.

Each classroom has a number above the door. 116 . . . 117. I start walking. Shouts and laughter from the playground float in through an open window. The windows are in a long row near the ceiling, so I can't see outside. That's okay with me because it means the kids on the playground can't see me either. I'm really not ready for this.

The tunnel feeling comes back. My legs want to stop walking, but I push myself forward. I just need to find my classroom and blend in when they all come through the door.

One . . . two . . . three . . . four. I count each step to distract myself. When I get to twenty, I look down at my paper again. *Great.* I was gripping it so hard it's now half-crinkled. That'll make a good first impression.

Mr. Garcia, Room 127. There it is—two doors ahead and on the right. I trudge my way forward and peek inside.

A guy in a tie stands behind a metal desk with a big wooden desktop. He taps a stack of papers on its surface. Let me guess. A worksheet due tomorrow asking for everything I haven't learned over the past three weeks.

He looks up. "Morning! Are you looking for someone?"

I look down at my paper. "Mr. Garcia?"

"That's me."

I step inside. It's a big classroom. Half the room has desks, arranged into four groups of six. The other half has a giant rug, a rocking chair, and a few bean bags. I see some plants, a goldfish in a small bowl, and a bunch of stuff about books and reading on the walls. "I'm Roisin. Row, like what you do on a boat, and then the word *sheen.*" I figure if I tell him now, maybe he'll say it right when he takes attendance later. The way a new teacher says my name on the first day always seems to stick, even when it's wrong. And it's almost always wrong.

I hand him the crinkled paper. "The office told me to give this to you."

"Welcome to Room 127! We've been expecting you." He walks over to a group of desks and points to one at the end. "This is your station. You're welcome to put your supplies inside. It's yours for the rest of the year."

Sure. If we stay that long.

"Thank you." I sit at the desk, unzip my backpack, and pull out two half-used notebooks, five worn folders, six sharpened pencils held together by a rubber band, one-third of a glue stick, and a bunch of markers in their original cardboard box with the top torn off. I asked Mom not to bother buying new supplies every time we move. They just stand out when I start in the middle of the year.

Each desk has a student's first name taped on top, written out in big letters on a piece of paper made to look like a book cover. Everyone else's looks a little worn. Mine looks shiny and new. ROISIN.

Mr. Garcia looks at his watch. "The rest of the gang should be joining us in about three minutes. I'll introduce you to the class right after the announcements. Would you like to say anything?"

"No thanks." The words tumble out before I can even think. *I might not have to introduce myself?* This day is looking better already.

"Okay," says Mr. Garcia. "No problem. New students give an introduction at their first assembly anyway, so you'll have a chance to say a more formal hello then." He gives me a reassuring nod and then returns to his desk.

My day becomes way better and way worse, all at the same time. Knowing I don't have to introduce myself this morning lightens my mood exponentially. But the idea of introducing myself at the next assembly? In front of the *entire* school? I force myself to stop thinking about it because passing out on the first day is not a good look.

A loud, harsh bell rings over the intercom and makes my head hurt. Kids are coming down the hall, and I just need to make it through today.

The class starts walking in. Two girls stare at me. One is wearing torn jeans with a tie-dyed t-shirt. Her shiny, straight blonde hair sits perfectly at her shoulders. The other has these smooth black leggings with a bright white shirt and a denim jacket. Her brown hair is pulled into two perfect braids. I reach up to feel the top of my own head. Frizzies everywhere.

The one in denim points at me and whispers something to the one in the tie-dyed shirt. They both laugh. I bite my lip and pretend not to notice. I wish

I could shrink down and make myself so small no one would notice me.

The two girls walk across the room and take a seat at the station where I'm sitting. I want to get up and run. Instead, I pretend to study a poster on the wall beside me. The one in the tie-dyed shirt sits at a desk marked *Olivia*. The other sits at a desk marked *Paige*. Two more names for my popular girls collection. Three boys join the pod too. After a few minutes, when Mr. Garcia isn't looking, Olivia gives me a quick look, rolls a pencil across the table, and whispers, "Hey, Poodle Hair! Fetch!"

I stare down at her pink sparkly notebook and fidget with my hands under the table. *Don't cry. Do. Not. Cry.* I look up and force out a laugh. "Good one!" One thing I've learned from my four big brothers is not to let people know when they get to me. It only makes things worse. At least I know my brothers have my back when it really matters. Can't say the same about Paige and Olivia.

Paige laughs. One of the boys does too.

"Knock it off, Paige!" says a kid sitting across from me. His bright blue eyes get narrow and annoyed as he glares at her. They get a little wider when he turns and gives me an apologetic grin. The nameplate on his desk says Diego. His curly dark hair falls to the the top of his light gray hoodie. "Sorry," he says. "Just ignore her."

"Thanks," I whisper. My heart starts to slow

down. Most new schools have at least one kid like Diego. I wonder if people like him have any idea what a difference they make just by being nice.

Mr. Garcia stands in front of the whiteboard with a blue marker in his hand. "Good morning, everyone! Welcome back." He writes two words on the board: *Favorite Holiday.* "Today's warm-up question," he says. "You have five minutes."

The confusion on my face must be pretty obvious because Diego explains. "He does this every morning. Writes something on the board and asks us to 'talk amongst ourselves' at the table to warm up for answering discussion questions later."

Olivia twirls a strand of her perfect blonde hair. "Well, obvs, it has to be Christmas, right? I mean, last year, my parents gave me a new phone and my grandma basically gave me a whole new wardrobe. I guess I got a little more on my birthday, but since that's technically not a holiday, I'm sticking with Christmas on this one."

"I like Christmas, too," says Diego. "My abuelo comes to visit. She makes the best tamales."

"Tamales on Christmas?" asks Paige.

"Weird," says Olivia.

I'm almost mad enough to say something to her, but Diego just shrugs his shoulders like he doesn't need her approval and turns to me instead. "Do you have a favorite holiday?" he asks.

My mind starts to spin like somebody pointed

a remote at me and pressed double speed. *Should I mention Gran and her soda bread to show solidarity with Diego? I could say St. Patrick's Day. But the Fourth of July is also pretty cool. If I talk about fireworks, will Paige and Olivia think it's juvenile?*

Olivia points to the name on my desk. "How do you even *say* that? Raisin? Is your middle name Bran? Was your mom obsessed with cereal or something?"

That's a new one. Points to her for creativity, I guess. I squeeze my hands together under my desk and try to control the look on my face. Really wish there was some kind of escape hatch in the floor right now.

Diego gives her another glare. "Seriously, Olivia?" He looks at me and shakes his head. "Just ignore her."

I take a deep breath, clear my throat, focus on Diego, and find the words I've said about a thousand times. "By the way, it's Roisin. *Row,* like you do in a boat, and then *sheen. Row-sheen.*"

"Roisin," says Diego. He says it slow, in a way that tells me my name will be safe with him. He looks at the wall like he's thinking for a second, then nods. "That's nice. I like it."

The rest of the day goes a lot like the morning did. Diego must have a different lunch than I do because I don't see him anywhere in the lunchroom. I grab my tray and find a spot at the end of a full table and try to blend in. It seems to work. No one even notices when I tip my carton too high and spill chocolate milk down my chin. After lunch, I try my locker combination seven times before I give up and ask someone from the office for help. By the time we get all that straightened out, recess has ended. *Bonus!* A one-day reprieve from standing around the playground trying not to look awkward. How long will it take to find friends this time?

Will I even *make* friends this time?

At the end of the day, I find an empty seat on my bus and stare out the window. My stop is the last one, so I know it's going to be a while. The bus fills up until hardly any seats are left. Three guys hop on, laughing and wrestling with each other as they walk up the steps. The driver tells them to calm down. They walk down the aisle, and two of them smash in next to each other in the empty seat across from me. The other guy sits right next to me and acts like I'm not here. I hug my backpack to my chest.

The kid next to me yells "Incoming!" and fake punches his friend in the seat across from us. In the process, he elbows me in the shoulder. It stings a little. He looks back at me, shrugs his shoulders, and gives his friend another fake punch.

I scoot closer to the window, rub my shoulder, turn my head to look outside, and whisper "ouch." I don't even know why I say it. It's not like anyone cares.

When I finally get off the bus, a kid from my desk pod zips by on his bike and barks at me like a dog. *Very funny,* I think, vowing to never, ever pull my frizzy red mess into pigtails again. As first days go, this one was a real winner.

Oh, good. Mom's car isn't here. I almost forgot she's on an overnight business trip until tomorrow. It's okay with me because the last thing I want to do is dodge questions about my day. Gran will probably be home, but at least she knows enough to wait until I'm ready to talk.

Gran meets me at the door with a plate of homemade cookies. Chocolate chip and snickerdoodle. My favorites. "Here you go," she says. "I'm sure it's been a long day."

"Thanks, Gran. You're the best." I grab two warm cookies. "I'm going to the computer room to do homework." I always turn stuff in on time. It's one of the only things at a new school I can actually control.

Before I claim the computer, the boys barge in. They're at a different school, so they take a different bus. Joe and Patrick start a thumb war as soon as they walk through the door. Connor darts around them, grabs a cookie, and takes over the computer room by kicking off his shoes and dumping his backpack on the ground. He sits down at the desk. Aidan takes off his shoes and socks. Then, just for fun, he waves one of his long, smelly sweat socks in front of my face:

"Mmmm! Good!" he teases.

I swat the sock away and bolt up the stairs. "Come on, Roisin!" Aidan yells after me. "Sorry! It's just a joke."

I run down the hallway to my new room. "My whole life is a joke," I whisper. I pull the door hard to slam it, then catch it just in time. A slam would bring Gran up here to investigate. I really just want to be alone.

I set the cookies on my dresser, pull the pigtail holders from my hair, throw them on my dresser, and squeeze both pigtails tight. I toss my head from side-to-side to free my long, red, frizzy curls. Why even try to tame them?

I shove a snickerdoodle in my mouth, then grab my math homework and sit at my desk. It's pushed up against the wall, a couple of feet from an old-time radiator that likes to randomly hiss at me every few hours. One of many things I already know I won't miss when it's time to leave this place. Math is usually my favorite subject, but after staring at the same problem for five minutes, I give up. It's hard to get my brain to learn anything new when I'm just worried about what fresh insults Paige and Olivia will have for me tomorrow. My desk chair scrapes on the wooden floor as I push myself back and look around the room.

I need my fidget box. I'm sure I packed it before the move. It holds a neon Slinky from my

Christmas stocking last year, a squishy mini football from a giveaway at one of my brother Joe's games, and a balloon-thing filled with rice that Mom brought home from a tradeshow. Maybe keeping my hands busy will help. But where is it?

One lonely, unpacked moving box sits in the corner. I drop it on my bed and pick at the packing tape until I get enough of a grip to peel it off the top. I ball up the crinkled tape and toss it in the garbage. The flaps pop up like the box is ready to burst. I push the flaps away and look inside.

Wait. This isn't my stuff. An old book sits at the top, strung together by yarn and topped with a worn leather cover that says "Clippings" in faded gold letters. It's a scrapbook. Gran said she wanted me to look at it a few weeks ago, but we never got around to it.

I pick up the book to set it aside, so I can return it to her later. The second I touch it, an electric tingle runs up my arm, kind of like someone just dumped a bucket of ice chips mixed with glitter from my fingertips to my elbow. I drop the book back in the box, then stare at my hand. It doesn't *look* any different.

Weird. I shake my head back and forth to get rid of this feeling, then try picking it up again. The electric tingle comes back. What *is* this thing?

I drop the book on my bed and flip it open to one of the first pages, a faded photo—or maybe a drawing, I guess. A mom and dad are standing by a ship, with six kids standing around them. The mom has a baby in her arms, but everyone else is holding a basket or a suitcase.

Whoa.

One of the sisters looks like me. *A lot like me—* all the way down to her unruly, frizzed-out hair. It's almost like I posed for one of those old-time photos or something. Now I'm really curious.

I pick up the scrapbook. The tingle happens again, this time a little lighter. I leave the book open as I carry it down the steps. The living room is empty, but I hear shouts and basketball bounces coming from outside. Curtains blow in the breeze as I look out the window.

No surprise—the boys are in the driveway playing two on two. Gran sits to the side on a lawn chair, being referee. I open the front door and head straight for her.

Joe elbows Aidan on his way to the hoop. "Foul!" shouts Gran.

"Ha!" Aidan laughs.

"Awww, Gran!" says Joe.

Gran notices the open scrapbook in my hands. Her eyes get wide. She stands. "Time out!" she calls.

I point to the girl in the drawing. "Who is this?"

Gran smiles. "You're on your own, boys," she says.

Her eyes twinkle as she glances at me, then

points to the open page in the scrapbook. "That's your great-great-great-great grandmother, Roisin the First. Come inside. I'll tell you more."

I follow Gran to the living room. We sit side-by-side on the couch, the scrapbook shared across both our laps. "Roisin the First?" I ask. "She kind of looks like me."

Gran studies the photo. "Indeed."

"Do you know much about her?"

"I do," answered Gran. "I first saw a scrapbook like this one when I was about your age. Mama had it in a box for safekeeping, and one day, she pulled it out to share with me. She told me all about the photos. The one we're looking at now was a drawing from the *Illustrated London News* when they did a story on people leaving Ireland for America. A friend saw it in the paper and sent it to them after they arrived here."

I study my great-great-great-great grandmother's face in the photo. I turn a few of the pages and find more photos of Roisins—some in color, and some in black-and-white. My own baby picture is on the very last page.

"So, these are the Roisins?"

"Yes," answers Gran.

"Can you tell me about them?"

"Tell you about them?" asks Gran, green eyes shining. "Oh, my dear Roisin. I can do better than that."

Gran flips to the first page of the scrapbook, then reaches for my hand. She hovers it over the open page and gestures for me to press down on the book. I feel my fingers tingle.

"Whenever you're ready, dear."

"Ready? For what?"

Gran puts her arm around me and nods at the scrapbook. "To find your place in a grand adventure."

What is she talking about?

Gran gives my shoulders a squeeze. I take a deep breath, suddenly feeling brave. I'm not sure where that's coming from, but I guess I'll take it. Whatever this adventure is, something inside me is telling me it's time.

The page pulls at my hand like a magnet. With Gran's help, I stretch out my fingers, close my eyes, and press my open hand on the page. The tingling travels up my arm, then swirls around me like a blast of cool air on a hot summer day. The brave feeling fades a little, but it's too late to turn back now.

I open my eyes, and I'm not in the living room anymore.

Chapter Two: Roisin the First

1845

Moooooo.

What is that sound? I spin around and try to take in everything around me all at once. A brown and white cow stands right next to me in a field, chomping on grass. I back up a little. She seems way too interested in eating to even notice me, but I don't know much about cows, and I'm not taking any chances.

Across the field, I notice a little white house with a roof that looks like it's made out of hay or something. The house is next to a bright green hill. I've never seen that shade of green before—vivid, soft, and fuzzy. I wish I could reach far enough to touch it. Wherever I am, it smells like rain.

I close my eyes hard and keep them closed for a second to check if I'm dreaming. When I open them again, everything is the same. Is this really happening?

Minutes ago, I was sitting in the living room with Gran. Now, I'm in the middle of a strange place, standing next to a cow, stuck inside a fence made of big, round stones. I think about running—but where would I even go?

To calm down, I focus on the bright green hill and picture myself sitting next to Gran on the sofa. Her words come back to me. *To find your place in a grand adventure.* I take a deep breath. The brave feeling returns a little. "I can do this," I tell myself. Besides, something about this place feels a little like—home.

The door to the house flies open, and a girl about my age runs straight at me. The urge to run rises up again. Should I be worried? *Wait.* Hair tied back. Frizzy curls flying everywhere. Kind of looks like—me.

This is the same girl from the first page of Gran's scrapbook!

I force myself to stay put, and the girl catches up to me. "Hello!" she says, a little out of breath. "I am Roisin the First, also known as Roisin Katherine Murphy of the wee town of Spiddal in County Galway, Ireland. And since you're holding the book, I know *you* must be a Roisin." She stops, looks me over, and thinks for a second. "Roisin the Seventh!" she concludes. "Very pleased to meet ye."

Thoughts tumble through my head like some kind of thunderstorm. She's Roisin the First? How does she know who I am? Where am I? *When* am I?

Unbelievable.

"Um, h—hello," I manage to say. "How. . . how did I get here?"

"Well, that's easy. 'Tis the book. When she's ready, each Roisin takes her first journey to meet the grandmothers that came before her. Now, don't worry yourself. When you're ready to move on, all you must do is turn to a new page, and you'll land someplace else near a Roisin. During your travels, the Roisins will know ya right away, and only the Roisins can see or hear ya. When you leave, they'll remember you, but they won't remember anything you've said. After all, knowing the future could change the present, and we can't have that now, can we?"

Wow. And I thought our vacation to Orlando was cool.

"Come along!" says Roisin the First. "We must be on our way. Da's about to tell his stories." I follow her as she rushes to a gate made of thick tree branches, unlatches it from the other side, and pushes. The gate creaks as it opens. She tugs on my hand to pull me to the other side and then latches the gate again. "This way!"

A couple raindrops hit my face as we run across the field and into the house. I barely have time to think, but it feels like all the good stuff from every Christmas and birthday and all the nerves from every first day at a new school, all rolled into one. "Don't worry, now," Roisin whispers to me just before she opens the door. "No one inside can see ya."

The outside air is wet and chilly, but as soon as she opens the door to the little white house, warm air rushes out. Someone must have just said something funny because everyone inside seems to be laughing. Roisin's mom rocks in a wooden chair, needle and thread in her hands, sewing some kind of dress. I find a spot in the back corner of the kitchen and take a seat on a worn wooden bench. On the other side of the room, Roisin sits cross-legged on the floor next to her brothers and sisters. One, two, three, four, five, . . . six kids! Their dad stands in front of the fire telling a story. Soon, he's galloping around the room, singing about a hero on a magic horse.

If my dad ever did something like that, I would wonder if aliens had taken over his brain. But somehow, inside this place, with no screens and only the fireplace for light, these stories seem like the most natural thing in the world.

He stops galloping, crouches down next to Roisin and her brothers and sisters, and turns his voice to a whisper. I want to move closer so I can hear him better. Roisin the First *did* say no one else could see me, but the idea seems so strange. Is it true?

I move a little closer to one of Roisin's little

brothers, then freeze. Finally, I build up the courage to wave a hand in front of his face. I hold my breath. Nothing. No response. Roisin gives me a quick smile and a nod.

Finally confident only the other Roisin can see me, I step a few feet forward to hear the rest of the story. Everyone is quiet now, except for Roisin's dad. "And that is how Setanta escaped to the forest, where he laid his head upon a pillow of soft fallen leaves and dreamed until morn."

Roisin's mom stands from her rocking chair. "And just like our hero Setanta, you too must rest now, wee ones."

One of the little kids lets out a loud yawn. Roisin stands and helps her mom pull quilts from a chest under the window. The two of them work together to spread a big patchwork one out on the floor.

Roisin's youngest brother runs to the quilt and plops down on the middle of it with a soft thunk. He yawns, rubs his eyes, and shouts "Good night!" The older kids giggle. Roisin's mom takes another blanket from the wooden chest and tucks it around him. "Say your prayers, child," she whispers, then kisses him on the forehead.

Roisin and her brothers and sisters snuggle in around him until all of them have a spot on the cottage floor. None of them have their own rooms—or even their own beds. But somehow, it doesn't seem to matter.

Roisin looks around to make sure no one is watching, then gives me a good night wave. She closes her eyes, and before long, she's snoring. Another thing we have in common, I guess.

What now? It's dark, but there's no way I could sleep with all the thoughts swirling around in my head. I carry the Book of Roisins over by the fire where I can see better. The next page is the picture of a ship Gran and I had looked at together before all this started.

I don't know about this. I turn to the photo of me at the end of the book. Maybe I should just go home.

I use the glow of the fire to look around the small cottage, then think back on the day.

No. I'm not ready to go home yet. I don't know much about what's happening on the next page of the scrapbook, but I'm pretty sure no one named Paige or Olivia will be there. My heart beats a little faster. Time for another adventure.

I turn back to the photo of the ship, hold a hand over it, spread out my fingers, close my eyes, and press my palm against the page. The tingling starts, then the cool breeze—until I'm not inside the cottage anymore.

~~~~~

Yuck. What is that smell? Wherever this is, I'm pretty sure somebody just barfed.
~~~~~

It's hard to see in this place, and everything is rocking. I hug the scrapbook to my chest. Maybe it *is* time to open the last page and go back home. Something jolts. I fall sideways and bump into some kind of rounded wall. I lean against it and lock my feet in place to steady myself.

Finally, my eyes adjust to the light. I see rows of small bunk beds, stacked three to four high. Almost everyone is sleeping. It must be the middle of the night here. I squint to see a little better and notice Roisin the First and her family in bunks just across from me. Everything jolts again, hard.

"No!" cries out one of Roisin's little sisters. She's lying on the bunk below Roisin's.

Roisin leans her head down from over the bunk to check on her. "There now, Cara," she says. "It's only some rough waters. We'll be through them soon enough." Roisin is trying to sound strong, but her words still sound a little shaky.

"I'm scared," Cara says, voice so quiet I can hardly hear her.

Roisin sits up in her bunk, rubs her eyes, and slides down to the floor. She crouches next to Cara and leans in to whisper something in her ear. Cara sniffles and nods. Roisin climbs in the bunk next to her.

I strain a little to hear them against the loud crashing sounds coming from outside. "Rest, now," says Roisin. "The seas will calm. Besides, we'll all be in America before you know it." She takes a deep breath and starts humming a song to Cara that sounds like a lullaby.

America. I knew Mom's family came from Ireland, but I never knew this is how they got here. I must be on a ship. I feel another jolt, then slide down against the wall until I'm sitting on the floor. Roisin the First didn't see me when she woke earlier, and I'm not about to leave without talking to her. I repeat Roisin's words in my mind. *The seas will calm.* My eyelids feel heavy. I focus on the soft sound of Roisin's lullaby and feel myself drifting off to sleep.

~~~~~

The next thing I know, someone is tapping me on the shoulder. My eyes open, fast and wide. I'm so relieved to see Roisin the First standing next to me.

"Oh, good!" I tell her. "You can see me now. I saw you last night when everything was rocking. You were so brave. Where are we? And what's with all the bunk beds? I should show this to Connor and Aidan when they complain about not having enough space in their room!"

I reach out to hug her, but then remember that even though people can't see me, they *can* see her, and it probably wouldn't be good for her to look like she's giving some kind of imaginary hug. She locks eyes with me, nods her head to the side toward a little nook a few feet down, then turns and starts walking. Even without words, I know I'm supposed to follow.
~~~~~

I take two steps and nearly fall over. It's hard for me to balance because the ship keeps rocking. Roisin the First seems used to it.

A few lanterns make it lighter down here now, but it's still like walking down the hall at midnight with just a nightlight to see. Only a few people are left sleeping. Some kids are sitting crisscross applesauce on the floor, playing a game with dice. Next to them, a lady sits on the edge of one of the bunks, holding a baby wrapped in an old blanket. Everything jolts again. The lady hugs the baby closer. I lean against a bunk to stop myself from face-planting.

I take a few more steps and hear someone groan. I turn my head to see a guy who looks like a grandpa. He rubs his hand across the forehead of an older lady lying in one of the bunks. "There, there," he says. "Close your eyes and rest now, Molly. The sleep will do you good." She has bright red cheeks. It reminds me of the way my brothers look after they come home from sledding. But she doesn't look cold. Her forehead has sweat on it. She looks heated. Really heated. The man with her looks worried. I hope she'll be okay.

We keep walking between the stacks of bunk beds, and I realize there aren't any windows. No wonder it's so hard to see. People are everywhere. It's like someone moved a school assembly to somebody's basement, turned off the lights, and made everyone stay for a really long time.

Finally, we get to a corner where no one can see Roisin. I hug her tight. "I've never been so happy to see someone! Can you tell me about this place?"

Roisin frowns and wrinkles her nose. "We're in *steerage,*" she says, "down in the bottom of a sailing ship, on our way to a place called America."

Roisin's forehead creases. "Something terrible happened back home. They call it *the hunger.*" She stops talking, but I know her head is full of thoughts. I can see it in her eyes. She takes a deep breath, and the words tumble out. "All across Ireland, the potatoes turned black in the ground. We had no food and no money to pay the landlord. Da said we must find a new place to live, or surely we would all starve. He sold our cow and our pigs to pay for passage."

I think of the green hill, the white house, and the stone fence. I imagine someone leading the cow out of the field and away from home. Maybe Roisin is thinking about something like that too because she looks like she's about to cry. Instead, she clears her throat, swipes a tear away with the back of her hand, holds her head up a little higher, and lets out a shallow breath. She nods and gives me a small half-smile. I know that look because it's the same one I get when I'm trying to convince myself everything will be okay.

"Are you scared?" I whisper.

She shakes her head *no*, but she's not very

convincing.

"Really?"

Roisin tilts her head up, like the answer is somewhere on the ceiling. When she looks back down, her eyes are wet again.

"Truth be told, yes." Roisin's voice is strained and quiet. "When the storms come, the ship tosses about like a stone skipping across the water. And so many people have fallen ill. One man played the fiddle nearly every night for us. Last week, he died. His wife was so very sad. Near the start of our journey, me own Da was sick for days. Mam wouldn't let us near him. She didn't want us to catch it. Thank the Lord, he recovered." She pauses. "And I miss our home in County Galway and our stories by the fire."

So many questions toss through my head. I think of how hard it is for me to move someplace new. And I never had to cross an ocean. "What happened to your cottage?" I ask. "Is someone living there now?"

"I don't know. The landlord will decide. But if someone moves in, I hope they're good to me grandmam and grandad next door."

"They lived next to you?"

"Yes." Roisin gets a faraway look, and I can tell she's picturing them.

"And they decided to stay?"

"Yes. Grandad wouldn't leave the land. It's all

he's ever known. We left them with enough money for passage here, and I can only hope they'll use it if they need it. They might be okay with only two mouths to feed and a milking cow and two pigs left. Much more than most have right now." Roisin stopped, looked down at the ground, and then looked up again. "Our neighbors, the O'Connor's, came to our door for food just a week before we left. Wee Mary had green around her mouth. She had so much hunger she tried to eat grass. I pray for them every day."

I think of Gran and how it would feel if we moved so far away that I wasn't sure I'd ever see her again. My heart feels heavy. I don't know what to say. "I'm sorry" is all that comes out.

"Thank you."

"You're so brave."

She clears her throat and pulls her shoulders back. "I know now I can be scared and brave, all at the same time. And when I'm brave, it helps the wee ones know they can be brave, too. Besides, it's been over five weeks on this ship, and Mam says we'll be in America soon."

Scared and brave, all at the same time. I've never quite thought about it that way, but it makes a lot of sense. I still don't have any words for her, so I just reach out and give her another hug.

Someone shouts for Roisin. We both peek around the corner. Her mom, dad, brothers, and sisters are all lined up by the stairs.

"We're allowed out of steerage for one hour each day, and now's our time. Would you like to come along?"

"One hour?" I look around this dark place. "You're only allowed out of here for *one hour*?"

Roisin nods. "Yes, and I won't be wastin' it!"

She peeks her head around the corner again and shouts to her mother. "I'm over here, Mam! I'll gather me shawl and meet you on deck." Roisin's mom nods. Her parents lead the little ones up the stairs.

Roisin grabs her shawl from her bunk. Together, we walk up steep stairs and into the sunlight on deck. The fresh air is damp and heavy, like at home when I walk out on the front porch after a thunderstorm. It smells like rain and salt and fish, all mixed together.

Up on deck, things look a little different. Across from us, some ladies in bright, fancy dresses stand around holding little matching umbrellas over their heads. I think they're called *parasols*. I saw them in a museum on a field trip once. The ladies are smiling and laughing like they're on vacation or something.

"Wow," I say. "Do they always get this dressed up for their hour on deck?"

Roisin shrugs her shoulders. "They can spend all the time they'd like on deck. Mam says they have a different kind of ticket than we do."

One of Roisin's littlest brothers takes off running and almost steps on one of the ladies' fancy lace-up boots. Roisin's mom gasps and dashes after him.

The lady lets out a little shriek, then gets a look on her face like she just sucked on a lemon. She glances over at Roisin's mom without really looking at her. "Control your offspring," she says, "or I shall be forced to speak with the captain about allowing vagrants on deck."

Roisin's brother giggles as his mom scoops him up and walks away without looking back. I scowl at the lady and wish she could see me. One of the older kids in Roisin's family is ready to do more than just scowl. He starts marching toward the lady when his mom grabs his wrist and gives him a firm look that says *absolutely not* without using a single word. My mom has one of those looks, too. They must learn it in mom school or something.

"But Mam," he says. "How can we let her talk to us like that?"

Roisin's mom smooths her skirt and holds her head up. Her cheeks are red, and her forehead is wrinkled. She clears her throat. "We know who we are, dear ones. No one's words can change that. Come along. Let's explore the other side of the deck today." Her voice shakes once, but she still sounds sure and steady. I spin around to follow Roisin and her siblings. *We know who we are.* I store those words in my memory.

Roisin and I follow her family to the other side of the deck. I hear a flapping sound and look up to see one of the ship's giant white sails moving back and forth in the wind.

Suddenly, it seems like everyone on board starts talking at the same time. "America! Ahead!" someone yells.

People turn to look at the shore in the distance. Roisin's dad runs toward us, a huge smile taking over his expression. "Come along, Murphy family! We must be gathering our things."

Roisin's jaw drops, and her eyes twinkle. She stretches her arms out and twirls around to celebrate. "I must go!" she says. "We're here! We're actually here!"

I'm so happy for her that I want to jump around like my brother Patrick does when his football team makes a game-winning touchdown. I'm not sure what to say until the perfect phrase pops into my head.

"Ádh mór ort!" I tell her. Those words have more meaning now.

My wish makes her smile even bigger. I wave goodbye and watch her run across the deck to her family.

She grips hands with two of her little sisters, and they follow her parents back down the steerage steps. Up and down the steps, back and forth across the deck, people are running in all different directions. It feels like time to move on.

I lean against a wall on the deck and open the Book of Roisins to the next page, a photo of a man and a woman standing by one of those covered wagon things we studied in history.

Time for another adventure. Just like Roisin, I'm feeling brave and scared, all at the same time— and maybe that's okay for now.

I stretch my fingers out, take a deep breath, close my eyes, and press my palm to the page. My arm feels tingly again, and the cool breeze swirls around me.

When I open my eyes, I'm not on the ship anymore.

Chapter Three:

Roisin the Second

1878

I don't think I'm on a ship anymore, but everything still feels like it's rocking. I hold a hand out to the side, take a deep breath, and close my eyes until I feel steady again. The air here is dry. Really dry.

I'm standing on some kind of path made of squished grass and dirt. It's definitely out in the country. No buildings. Just tall, dry grass and a bunch of trees. It's so hot I feel like I'm getting a sunburn just standing here. If Mom were with me, she'd have the sunscreen pulled out of her purse and opened by now. We give her kind of a hard time for her sunscreen obsession, but I sure could use some here. I wish I could see a Roisin right away because this place feels lonely. It's like the first day at a new school, except instead of being surrounded by a bunch of strangers, there's not a person in sight. I'm not sure which one is worse.

I squint up at the bright sky and see just one small cloud, nowhere near the sun. If I want shade, I'm going to have to find it myself. A towering tree across the path from me looks like it might work. Just as I head that way, a huge fly buzzes right by my face. A horse's whinny makes me jump and spin around.

Behind me, a covered wagon like the one in the scrapbook is parked by a big oak tree. How did I miss that? I guess I was so focused on finding shade I forgot to turn around. The wagon looks like one I saw on a field trip my class took to a history museum a few schools ago. Two big horses are standing beside it. My heart skips a beat when I realize there's a lady staring right at me.

She's wearing a sunhat, with a few frizzy red curls sticking out from under it. Even from a distance, her freckles are really standing out in this sun.

There she is! Another Roisin.

The knots in my stomach start to untwist. Maybe I'm not so alone after all. Her eyes shift to my scrapbook, and her face lights up. "What a grand surprise!" she says. "You surely do have good timing." She rushes to my side. Her long brown skirt swooshes with every step. "I am Roisin the Second. My husband Erik and I left New York a few months ago. Erik's brother and his wife staked some land for us out west. We're all going to be neighbors, but first, Erik and I must make our way there. Other than Erik and a few critters, I haven't seen a single living soul for days."

I understand how this works now, so I reach out to shake her hand. "Nice to meet you! I'm Roisin the Seventh."

She laughs with relief as she pulls me in for a hug, then backs up to look me over. "Indeed you are! Well, welcome to the prairie, Roisin the Seventh. I'm only sorry I can't offer you better weather for your visit. I'm afraid the heat has been dreadful this week."

"I was just looking for some shade before I saw you." I can't help staring at the wagon. Do they actually *live* in there?

Roisin notices me looking at it. "I'm sorry," I tell her. "It's just—it looks like something out of my history book."

She seems a little surprised. "So these made the history books, did they?" She points near the bottom of the wagon. "When Erik returns, we'll take the wheels off to soak in the river. When it gets hot like this, the heat will ruin them if we don't care for them properly."

"You have to take the wheels off? Every day?"

I think back to when we got a flat tire on the way to my aunt's house. It was a big deal and took almost all afternoon to get repaired. Imagine having to do that all the time.

Roisin looks a little amused at my question. "Well, not *every* day, but when the sun shines like this, we do. Would you like to see inside the wagon?"

"Yes, please!"

"Follow me. Erik went to the river to fish us some supper. We usually make due with the rations we packed, but we both decided it was time for a treat. He'll be back soon. I best get what I need to start cooking."

Along with her long brown skirt, Roisin is also wearing long sleeves and laced-up boots. She must be roasting in those clothes! I wish I could hand her a pair of flip-flops. For now, though, I can't wait to see what the inside of the wagon looks like. The sun beats down on my cheeks, and I can feel them turning red. At least the wagon will have some shade.

Out of nowhere, Roisin freezes and whisper-yells "Stop!"

The warning in her voice makes me seize up so fast I almost trip over my own tennis shoes. I feel my heart thumping, and I'm sweating even more than I was before. At first, the only thing I can hear is our breathing. Then I hear something else.

A rattle.

My eyes move in the direction of the sound, but

my body stays put. Did we just hear a snake? What would happen if one of us got bitten out here? It's not like we can call an ambulance. Or hop in the car and rush to the nearest hospital. "Is that what I think it is?" I gulp. The question comes out in a whisper, but not on purpose. It's all I can find of my voice.

"Indeed." Roisin points. She seems calmer now, so I feel my shoulders relax just a little. "The sound is coming from that rock over there. It must be where the little rascal has made its home. It won't bother us if we keep our distance. Here," she nods in a different direction, "let's go this way."

I close my eyes for a second and take a deep breath. The hot, dry air makes my throat a little scratchy. Roisin grabs my hand and struts forward, pulling me along like the whole rattlesnake thing never even happened. I look back to the place where we heard the sound. How fast can snakes move, anyway? I don't have much time to think about it, though, because before I know it, Roisin has taken me to the back of the wagon.

"How did you notice that sound?" I ask. "I didn't even hear it."

"Well, when you're out here, you learn to listen for things."

I re-think the flip-flops. Maybe her boots are a good idea after all.

She opens the flap on the back and gestures for me to step inside. I grab the edge to help pull myself in. It's a little stuffy in here, but cooler. The first thing I notice is a big rocking chair, tied sideways to the inside wall.

Roisin shrugs her shoulders a little. "I know it takes up a lot of space, but Da made it for me as a wedding gift before he knew we'd be taking this journey. I just couldn't leave it behind. Mam says I can think of them when I'm rocking my own babies someday. Erik and I will put it by the hearth when we build our home."

I move a little closer to the chair. Something about it seems—familiar. Then, I notice it. On the right armrest, just where the round part starts to curve down toward the seat, the initials CM are carved into the side. I've seen those letters before. I've seen this *chair* before. A shiver runs up my back. It almost seems unreal.

I reach out to touch it, then stop. I know this chair is extra special to Roisin. I need to ask first. "May I?"

"Of course."

I rub my hand over the initials, just like when Gran used to hold me in this chair. My finger follows the curved letters indented into the smooth wood. "These letters," I ask. "What do they stand for?"

Roisin looks a little proud. "Connor Magee. That's my Da. He carved the letters himself."

A thousand thoughts seem to run through my mind at the same time, but only one comes out of my mouth. "It's a sturdy chair," I tell her.

"Yes. It does seem to be. My Da is known as an excellent woodworker."

"I mean *really* sturdy." I look her in the eyes and try to figure out how to say this. She's not going to believe it. I mean, I barely do, and I've seen it with my own eyes. "My gran, Roisin the Fifth, has this chair in her bedroom. She used to rock me in it when I was little."

Roisin tilts her head, and her eyes get wide. She walks over to the chair and traces the letters herself this time. "Well," she says, almost in a whisper. "Isn't that grand?" When she looks up at me again, her eyes are a little watery. She pulls me in for a hug. "Thank you for your visit," she says. "I know I won't remember this detail about the chair after you leave, but it truly does mean the world to me now."

"Me too," I tell her. I really mean it.

Roisin clears her throat and shakes her head a little. "Okay," she says. "I must prepare for dinner." She opens a wooden box and pulls out a heavy, black frying pan.

"That's for the fish?" I ask.

"Indeed." Roisin the Second really seems to like that word. I like the way it sounds when she says it. Like she doesn't have a doubt in the world.

"Wow. At home, we cook our fish in the microwave."

She looks at me like I just spoke French or

something. "I don't believe I've heard of one of those."

Just as I'm trying to figure out how to explain what a microwave is, I hear a faint sound of yelling. Roisin jumps up, lifts the flap, and peers out the back of the wagon. "That's Erik!" she says. "We always stay within shouting distance from each other, just in case. Something's wrong."

A man in a cowboy hat is coming straight for us, running like he's trying to win a 100-yard dash or something. With one hand, he's holding down his hat. The other hand holds a fishing pole and a string with a bunch of fish on it, flapping against each other as he runs. "Roisin!" he yells. "Quick! We need the horses!"

Roisin glances at me. It's the same look as when we heard the rattlesnake, but even more urgent. "I'm sorry. I have to go! Come along if you'd like."

I want to help if I can, so I follow her as she jumps down from the wagon, runs to a tree where the horses are standing in the shade, and unties one of them. Both of the horses are so tall and strong. Roisin clicks her tongue and gives one of them a gentle pat on the side. "Come, Daisy," she says, her voice a mix of rushing and soothing as she leads the horse toward Erik. Daisy's soft brown hair glistens as she steps into the sunlight. I remind myself Erik can't see me, then follow right behind them.

Erik leans the fishing pole and the fish against

a tree. He runs to the wagon and jumps out moments later with two saddles in his hands. He gives one to Roisin. "I'll get Dandy ready if you can saddle up Daisy!" he shouts. "There's a family in trouble by the creek. Stuck wagon, with children inside." He looks around as he runs. "I don't like to be leaving our wagon out here alone, but it's not far, and they really need us."

Roisin grabs the saddle from the ground and puts it on the horse. "Do you want to come along?" she asks me.

I must be caught up in the moment because I nod yes before I even have time to think. When Dad was stationed in Kentucky, we lived next to a horse farm. Gran and I volunteered there. I feel my breath catch in my throat as I try to remember everything I learned. Roisin the Second takes a quick glance to make sure Erik can't see her, then helps me hoist myself onto Daisy's back.

Roisin hops up in front of me and grabs the reins. *Why did I say yes?* What if I slow things down for them? Maybe I should just get down and wait for them to come back.

My doubts stop there because Dandy dashes by us, carrying Erik on her back. "This way," he shouts. Roisin signals Daisy to follow, and we take off— fast! Even if I wanted to, there's no turning back now.

I remember Roisin the First's words back on

the ship. *Brave and scared, all at the same time.* If the other Roisins can do it, I can do it. I say a little prayer like Gran has taught me, then brace myself for whatever's next. I'm all in.

I hold tight to Roisin and feel the wind whip strands of my frizzy red curls across my face. Good thing Roisin's hair is tied up in a tight bun under her sunhat. Anything blocking her view would not be good right now. My body bounces up and down as we race forward. I feel my heart pounding to the rhythm of the horse's hooves.

Erik brings Dandy to a halt beside a wide creek. "Whoa!" coaxes Roisin. Daisy slows and carries us up next to them. Ahead, a big, covered wagon pulled by four horses is stuck in the middle of the creek. Two of the horses have made it to shore, but the two behind them are stuck in the water. Since I can't do any good from here, I slide down and run ahead to take a closer look.

The back of the wagon is surrounded by fast-flowing water that looks like it's about to start seeping into the wagon bed. The middle of the creek must be way deeper than it looks from the shore. The front of the wagon is in more shallow water, where a wheel is stuck in a deep spot in the mud. One of the horses tied to the wagon lets out an urgent, high-pitched whinny.

"Pa! I'm scared!" A girl peeks out from the covered part of the wagon. She looks and sounds like a preschooler.

The man on the bench spins back to look at her. "We'll be all right, child," he says. "Now go sit next to your ma. She and the baby need you."

"Sarah! Come here!" A woman's voice carries from the wagon, followed by a cry that sounds like my baby cousin when he was just two weeks old. There's a baby back there, too? What if the wheel breaks off? What if the whole wagon tips over? I try to take a deep breath again, but this time, the dry air just makes me cough. They must be so scared.

Roisin and Erik are working fast to harness Daisy and Dandy to the other horses in front of the wagon. When that's done, they stare at each other for just a second, eyes filled with a mix of worry and determination. I know the look. It's the one my parents gave each other a couple years ago when they had to tell us Dad was getting deployed.

Erik locks eyes with the man on the wagon's bench. "Ready?" he asks.

The man turns his head back to face the covered part of the wagon. "We've hitched some more horses, Margaret. Hold tight to the children. Are you ready?"

"Ready!" The woman's voice is strong, but I still hear it shake just a little.

"Ready, Pa!" shouts the preschooler. Roisin glances over at me, worry lining her forehead. Roisin and Erik only have two horses, and the wagon seems *really* stuck. What if the horses aren't strong enough? What if someone gets hurt? I hold my breath.

The man nods at Erik and raises the reins. "Haaaaa!" he shouts. The horses whinny and try to move.

"Come on, girls!" Roisin calls, standing beside Daisy. "We need you. *They* need you!"

Daisy and Dandy bear down and move ahead, slow and steady. The baby in the wagon starts to cry again. The stuck wheel spins, kicking up mud. "Come on, girls," I whisper, echoing Roisin the Second's message. "Ádh mór ort," I add, just for good measure. "You've got this!"

Daisy and Dandy lurch forward as the wheel escapes from the mud. The wagon bounces ahead, hard. The man on the bench reaches up to grab his hat before it goes flying off his head. He glances back at the wagon, "Margaret!" he shouts. "Is everyone all right?" He turns again to guide the horses as they haul the wagon up the hill. He pulls up on the reins and brings it to a stop.

"Margaret!" he shouts again, jumping off the bench and dashing to the back of the wagon. The baby cries again, even louder this time. That has to be a good sign, right?

He lifts the older daughter out from inside the wagon. "Pa!" she shouts, wrapping her arms around his neck so tight I wonder if he can breathe.

Roisin the Second is next to them in an instant.

"You're okay, Sarah," the man soothes. He sets her down next to Roisin. "Stay here!"

The baby is crying louder now. He runs back to the wagon, reaches up for the baby, and takes her from the mom. His eyes dart to Roisin the Second. "Ma'am could you help me, please?" She rushes to his side and takes the baby. "Shhhh," she soothes.

Finally, he helps the mom out of the back of the wagon. As soon as her feet hit the ground, she scans the shore for her children. Relief floods her face when she sees them standing by Roisin. She takes her husband's hand and heads toward them. "Thank you!" she tells Roisin. "I'll take them now."

Before Roisin can hand off the baby, the older sister wraps her arms around her mom's legs so fast that she almost knocks her over. The mom steadies them both, then reaches down with one hand to pat her older daughter's back. She makes her other hand into a cradle shape and nods to Roisin to let her know she's ready to take the baby. I feel so relieved for them.

Meanwhile, Erik has helped the man with the cowboy hat to calm the horses. The man shakes Erik's hand and reaches across with his other arm to grab Erik's shoulder. They stand like that for a few seconds. The man seems so grateful. He gives Erik a nod, then rushes to his family and surrounds them in a hug.

Roisin and Erik lead their horses away from the

others. When they stop, Roisin leans into him for a side hug. They watch the family in the distance and take just a few seconds for a deep breath. "We need to get back," Erik says, "to make sure our wagon's okay."

The wagon. I know there aren't a lot of people out here, but it would only take one dishonest person for all their stuff to be gone when they get back.

Wait! Speaking of stuff, I was so worried about getting on the horse on the way here that I left the Book of Roisins back at the campsite. What if someone has taken it? Would I be stuck here forever? My heart thumps like it might just pop right out of my chest. I have to remind myself to breathe.

I race up the shore and over to Roisin. While Erik's back is turned, she cups her hand to help me hoist myself onto the horse's back, then jumps up to join me. The hot, dry wind swooshes against us as Daisy gallops, following Erik as he steers Dandy forward. "The scrapbook!" I shout to Roisin. "I left it back with the wagon." Roisin nods to show she heard me. She can't shout anything back because Erik would hear her. My mind races. Will I ever see Gran again? What about Mom and Dad? And my brothers?

The warm, dusty air stings my eyes and makes them water. I squint ahead as we near the spot where we left. The wagon is still here! My eyes dart to the ground next to the tree where the horses were tied earlier. *There it is*—The Book of Roisins, lying safely in the shade of the towering tree. I try to tell Roisin, but the hot, dry air catches in my throat. I swallow hard and find my voice. "I see the book!" I shout.

We're almost there. Roisin pulls up on the reins to slow Daisy's pace.

Oh no! Ahead of us, Erik steers Dandy toward the tree, right in the path of the scrapbook. "Stop!" I scream. But it's no use. He can't hear me.

Roisin turns back to me. "It's okay," she whisper-shouts.

How can it be okay? The book I need to get home is seconds away from getting stomped into a thousand pieces. Nothing about that is okay. *Nothing.*

I wince as the horse's hoof comes down on the book. But then, something strange happens. The hoof goes right through book, like it's nothing but air. When the horse moves ahead, the book is still sitting there, just like it was before.

Erik hops off his horse and tethers her to the tree. She dips her head down into a wooden bucket under the tree and starts drinking. Erik pats her on the side. "You've earned it, girl!" he tells her. "I'll go check on the wagon and the fish," Erik says. "Before all this started, I caught a whole mess for dinner!"

"I saw," says Roisin. "What a treat! I'll get the fire ready."

Roisin waits until Erik is out of hearing

distance, then turns to me. "About the book," she says. "During your travels, the other Roisins are the only ones who can see or touch it. It's good to keep it close in case you need to leave quickly, but no damage will come to it. Or you."

Relief washes over me as I lift the scrapbook off the ground and pull it close for safekeeping. "Thank you," I tell her. "I'll never let it out of my sight again."

She reaches out to me. I drop one hand from the scrapbook and grip her hand.

"I must get dinner started. What a pleasure it has been to meet you, Roisin the Seventh. I've been missing Ma and my sisters, and seeing you surely is a delight. Please, rest here in the shade as long as you'd like. And do come see me again." She hugs me tight, then walks backward for a moment to keep an eye on me as she walks away. With a final smile and a wave, she turns and struts toward the wagon.

I watch her hop in the back of the wagon and think once again about the rocking chair tied to the side of it. For the first time in my life, I don't feel like the "only girl" anymore. Mom always tells me even though I don't have sisters, I still have *sisterhood*. I never understood what she meant until now.

Suddenly, I can hardly wait to meet the next Roisin. For the first time on this little adventure, I don't even consider turning to the last page and going back home.

The next page in the scrapbook has a picture of a lady standing by a train. She's wearing a long, simple skirt, a lace top that reaches up kind of like a turtleneck, and a fitted suit jacket to go over it. All business. Her red hair is tied back in a bun. I'd know her anywhere. Definitely a Roisin.

I give a quick glance back to Roisin the Second and Erik. I hope I get to come back someday. I'd love to see that rocking chair inside their new house. For now, though, new adventures are waiting—for all of us.

I lift my hand, stretch my fingers wide, and press down on the page. A gust of cold air swirls around me, until I'm not in the wagon anymore.

Chapter Four:

Roisin the Third

1913

Neeeighhhh!

Was that a horse? Is this a farm? I spin in a slow circle to take in everything around me. Nope. Definitely not a farm. I'm standing on the sidewalk beside a wide paved street. It's cold, but not freezing. I don't see a Roisin yet, so I do another slow spin to see what I missed. What is this place?

A bunch of people are standing around in the middle of the street. I notice a lot of women, but hardly any guys—except for a few men wearing long coats with shiny metal buttons up the middle and a police badge pinned on the side. One of them crosses his arms and scowls like he doesn't really want to be here. Do *I* want to be here? The vibe is a little tense. I hug the scrapbook to my chest and hope to see a Roisin. Soon.

My palms are sweating. My face feels flushed, like it's probably as red as a tomato. I drop one hand to my side and wiggle my arm a little to try to shake off this nervous feeling. *Remember, only Roisin can see you,* I remind myself. If only I knew where she was.

The whinny I heard earlier must have come from a pair of horses in front of a big wooden wagon parked on the side of the road. It's half-full of women, some standing and some sitting. They look a little dressed up. They're all wearing long skirts. Some have long-sleeved, button-up shirts with puffy sleeves at the shoulders. So many buttons! It would take me forever to get dressed if I had to wear that every day. They're also wearing laced-up, high-heeled boots that do not look comfortable at all. I look down at my feet and once again feel thankful for my regular old tennis shoes.

In the distance, I hear a few notes from a trombone, like when Connor is practicing in his room. With all the people in the street, I wonder if this is some kind of parade. It doesn't really feel light and fun like parades back home, though. Some people are smiling, but some are scowling. There's tension in the air. I look down at the scrapbook and remind myself I can leave any time I want. I'd really like to find Roisin before I leave, though. I scan the crowd again, looking closer this time.

There she is! Roisin is sitting on the wagon I saw earlier, staring straight at me. The red hair and freckles must give both of us away—although her curls are a little harder to see because they're sticking out from under a fancy hat. This Roisin looks a little older. If I had to guess, I'd say she's around 25 or so. She says something to the person sitting next to her, then stands up and hops down. After her feet hit the ground, she looks me in the eyes and bobs her head to one side as if to say "go this way."

Finally! Time for some answers.

When I turn to follow her, something in the distance at the end of the street catches my eye. Wait! Is that—The White House? As in, the place where The President of the United States actually lives?

Roisin is already out of sight in the space between two buildings. I definitely don't want to lose track of her, so I walk faster and find her standing in a narrow dirt alleyway. She grabs my hand and pulls me behind a concrete outdoor staircase where no one can see us. Then, she gives me a huge hug.

"You have no idea how good your timing is!" she tells me. "I'm Roisin the Third. So pleased to meet you! And forgive me, but first, I must ask you a question. I know I won't remember your answer, but just knowing for a few moments would be so very grand."

This Roisin sure doesn't waste any time. "Okay," I tell her.

"Can you vote?" She asks the question in a rush and waits for my answer like my brother Joe when he's super hungry and waiting for Gran to pull a tray of cookies out of the oven.

I shake my head *no*. Roisin's hopeful smile turns into an instant frown, and the light leaves her eyes. She looks down at the ground. "I see," she says softly.

"I mean, I can't vote yet because I'm not old enough. But Mom and Gran always take me along when they go."

Roisin looks back up at me. "Wait. You mean, your mom can vote? Your grandma can—" She pauses and puts her hands over her heart. Hope fills her voice. "Your mom and your grandma can *both* vote?"

I nod yes. Roisin tilts her head back and laughs, then claps her hands together. "Oh, that is most wonderful news!"

I look around to make sure we're still alone. Now it's my turn to ask some questions. "Where are we?" I ask.

"Washington DC," she answers. "Tomorrow is the inauguration of President Woodrow Wilson. Today, we're reminding him women should have the right to vote, and we're asking him to support us in our efforts to amend the US Constitution to give us that right."

We studied this in history. I search my brain for the word we learned to describe people who fought for this. It finally comes to me. Roisin the Third is a *suffragist.* Seriously, how cool is that? No wonder my answer was so important to her.

A bunch of different thoughts rush through my mind at once. First, I should probably thank her for what she's doing. Until now, I always kind of took it for granted I could vote. Second, the streets are so crowded! How many people are actually here for this thing? Also, I can't believe I'm in Washington DC. I've only seen pictures up to now, and I really want to explore this place.

"Do you live here?" I ask. "Do all these people live here?"

"No," says Roisin. "I came by train from New York with a friend. We're both nurses back home, so we're riding on a wagon with a group of other nurses. I've heard we also have schoolteachers, lawyers, marching bands, and people from all over the country and the world walking in this procession." She shakes her head. "It really is quite amazing!"

Sure is. I never really realized how many people had to fight to make this happen.

"I wish we could talk longer, but I must get back to the wagon," she says. "Would you like to walk me back?"

"Yes!" I don't even hesitate. There's so much

to see here.

"I was hoping you'd say that! A few more moments with you would be a treat indeed. Shall we?"

Indeed. There's that word again. Must be a Roisin thing.

"Lead the way!" I say. "And Roisin?"

She starts walking, then looks back at me. "Yes?"

I reach out to grab her hand. "Thank you." Those words don't seem quite enough, but they're all I have for now.

Tears brim in her eyes. "You are most welcome."

I follow her back through the narrow passageway between the buildings and watch as someone helps her back onto the wagon. I look down at the scrapbook. I usually leave right away after I'm done talking to a Roisin, but this Roisin has me feeling a little extra brave, and I want to see more.

I look down the street. Where does the parade start? If I could get to the front, maybe I could see the whole thing. I squeeze my way through the crowd for a few blocks. At first, I'm afraid of running into people, until I realize when people can't see me, they kind of pass right through me, kind of like the horse's hoof passed through the scrapbook when I was visiting Roisin the Second. I'm still not sure how all this works, but this invisible thing comes in handy.

After passing a few more horses and wagons, I notice some tracks in the middle of the road. A train car goes down those tracks every few minutes, carrying a bunch of people on it. The people in the street try to move out of the way, but it all seems a little chaotic. At home, they just block the whole road when we have a parade. Why didn't they do that here?

I suck in a breath and accidentally take in a bunch of cigar smoke floating through the air. It makes me cough, and I feel my eyes water. I look to see where it's coming from and notice a group of people standing far back on the sidewalk. A lot of them are guys, but not all of them. Some are smoking cigarettes and cigars. I notice a few of them glaring into the crowd, a little like the look Mom gets when I forget to do my chores, except way worse. I'm glad they can't see me.

Some police officers are standing between these people and the rest of the parade, but the officers are definitely outnumbered.

I pick up the pace and move closer to the street side of the sidewalk, as far away from the angry-looking people as I can get. Finally, I make it to the front of the parade lineup. I spy a raised wooden porch in front of one of the buildings and settle in there to see things a little better.

Near the front of the parade line, a lady sits on top of a white horse. She's wearing a long white cape that falls down over her shoulders and drapes over the back of the horse, too. She's also wearing a gold crown with a star, and her dark, curly hair falls down her back. She looks majestic up there.

I guess I'm not the only one who thinks that because a little girl standing near me asks, "Who is that, Mama?" She emphasizes the word *that,* as if the person is someone magical.

"That, my dear, is Miss Inez Milholland," says her mom. "Doesn't she look marvelous? Ms. Milholland is from Brooklyn, just like us. She is a lawyer, and she works hard to help ladies have fair working conditions. What a fitting person to help lead the procession!"

A minute or so later, the parade begins. Everything seems to be going great until I hear angry voices in the distance. It's getting so crowded I can barely see anything, so I move back down the sidewalk to try to find a better spot. That's when I notice it. A huge group of people trying to close in on the parade. I look down to make sure I still have the scrapbook, just in case I need to leave fast. But what about everyone else? Will they be safe? Will Roisin be safe? I'm really worried for her. My throat starts to feel a little tight. I swallow hard and try to take a deep breath.

The people move in closer, and I hear what they're saying.

"Go home where you belong!" yells one guy.

Someone else shakes her finger at the marchers, scowls, and screams "Disgraceful!" over and over again. Her face is red with anger and urgency, like she just ate a jalapeno or something.

A guy in a suit wearing a small black hat throws a half-eaten apple and hits one of the marchers in the arm. She rubs her arm but keeps her eyes ahead and still marches forward. Another marcher links arms with her, and they move a little faster, side-by-side. I feel my jaw clench. Where is Roisin the Third? I wish I could see her and know she's okay.

Someone else takes a half-smoked cigar out of his mouth and pitches it into the crowd like he's throwing a dart at a dartboard. I hear myself gasp, and I grip the scrapbook a little tighter. The cigar hits the side of a wagon and falls to the ground. I'm so thankful it didn't hurt anyone.

A lady next to me looks at one of the people dressed in a police uniform. "Can't you do something?" she asks.

He crosses his arms and shakes his head. "What would I do to make any kind of difference, lady? Maybe they shouldn't be out here in the first place. Did you ever think of that?"

I get a sick feeling in my stomach and start to open the scrapbook to go home, but I just can't get myself to do it. I need to make sure Roisin the Third is okay. I can see her wagon a couple of blocks down. It's way too crowded for me to go anywhere, so I climb the steps to a platform and watch from a distance.

The angry crowd keeps closing in until the parade is stuck in place. The marchers latch arms and stand together. My heart is beating so hard I can feel my pulse in my ears. Everything stays like this for a while. I keep squinting to try to catch a glimpse of Roisin on the wagon. So far, nothing.

After what seems like forever, some soldiers on horses start riding into the crowd. A policeman standing next to me looks relieved. "Looks like President Wilson called in the cavalry," he says out loud, to no one in particular. He straightens his posture and starts helping the soldiers move the crowd back.

Soldiers. Just like my dad. I wonder if Dad ever had to help push a crowd back. Gran always calls him "one of the good guys." This helps me understand what she means. I've always been proud of him, but now I'm a little extra proud. I wonder if the families of the cavalry soldiers move around a lot, like we do.

The people in the angry crowd are leaving. I close my eyes to shut out the world for a second, take a deep breath, and feel my whole body calm down. Roisin's wagon is finally free to make its way down the street. I angle my hand over my forehead to block the sun from my eyes and see just a little bit better.

The wagon gets closer. I'm suddenly thankful for our red hair because I know it will make her stand out so I can see her. As hard as I try to focus, though, it's too far away to make out anything specific. I've never had more trouble being patient in my entire life. I feel a little like I'm watching a slow-motion replay. The fading sounds of the angry group as the soldiers push them back even more. The claps and cheers of the people around me trying to support the marchers. The clip-clop of the horses' hooves on the pavement.

Finally, I have a better view of the wagon. *There she is!*

Roisin is standing near the edge of the wagon, and it looks like something might have made her hat fall off because her hair's a little messy. She's reaching up to pin the hat back on her head. Our eyes meet. I give her a nod. She's flustered, but she still manages to nod back at me.

I hop down to the sidewalk and jog along the side of the street to keep up with Roisin's wagon. Finally, it stops at the end of the route. I know I only met this Roisin a little while ago, but it takes *a lot* of willpower to stop myself from jumping up on that wagon and asking her if she's okay. The last thing she needs, though, is for someone to see and wonder why she's talking to some imaginary friend. I guess I'll have to wait my turn.

Roisin is talking to someone as she stands in line to step down from the wagon. I wonder if that's the other nurse from New York who came along with her. When they reach the road, Roisin gives me a quick glance and turns back to her friend. "There's something I need to take care of." She points to a corner just a block away. "Could I meet you down there in just a few minutes?"

"Of course," her friend says. "We still have some time before the train leaves. You're sure you're okay?"

"Yes," says Roisin. She looks at me for a second, then back at her friend. "Right as rain. If that angry gentleman thought a little old piece of fruit would make me give up this cause, then he clearly doesn't know me at all."

"No, he does not," her friend agrees. "All right then. I'll see you in a few minutes."

Roisin signals to a spot behind a building, and we head that way. Finally out of sight, I give her a giant hug. I can't help it. I'm just so glad she's okay.

"What happened?" I ask.

"Oh—someone in the crowd decided to waste a perfectly good apple by throwing it at my head. He must not have very good aim because it hit my hat instead. Knocked it right off my head. I'll admit it startled me at first. But the other ladies on the wagon were quick to help, and I was once again reminded I am far from alone in this fight." She stops and grasps my hand. "And you, Roisin the Seventh, are the perfect reminder of what we're fighting for. I must get back to my friend, but I'm so very thankful for your visit."

"I'm the one who should be thankful," I say. "You are amazing."

She waves at me, then turns to walk away. I watch her for a second and think of one last thing I want to tell her.

"Ádh mór ort!" I shout. She glances back at me with a determined smile, then disappears around the corner to meet her friend.

Whew. What a long day, and I was only watching! I can't imagine what it must be like to be one of the marchers. I wish I could go up to every single one of them and tell them what a difference they're going to make.

I open the scrapbook to the next page. Gran and I didn't get to this part together when we were talking about the book, but this Roisin is wearing some kind of old-time Army uniform. I'd really like to meet her, but now I'm tired. So tired. Plus, I have a few questions for Gran. Part of me wants to keep going, but deep down, I know it's time to go home.

I turn to the back page of the scrapbook, the one with the picture of me. By now, I know the drill. I open the page wider, spread out my palm, take a deep breath, and press my hand to the page. The rush of cold air swirls around me, until I'm not in Washington DC anymore.

Chapter Five

Present Day

I'm right back where I started, sitting on the couch in the living room with Gran, sharing the Book of Roisins between us. Gran reaches her arm around my shoulder and gives me a squeeze. "Welcome back," she says.

My head feels like our dryer looks after someone throws a bunch of wet clothes in it and presses *start*. So many thoughts are tumbling around so fast. I'm not sure what to say. "That was—I mean, I saw—." There's too much to say at once, so I just settle on one word. "Amazing."

"Indeed," says Gran. "You must have a lot of questions. I know I did when I was your age. Ask away.”

I let the words spill out as fast as I can say them.

“How much time went by while I was visiting the Roisins?”

“Just the few seconds it took for you to turn the first page,” says Gran. “Time stands still here while you’re away. Everybody just sort of freezes in place.”

“Can I go back? I really hope I can go back. I wanted to visit the next Roisin, but I was just so tired.”

Gran squeezes my hand. “Any time you want, dear one. For your first few trips, though, just be sure to talk to me or your mom before you go. We’ll help you decide if you’re ready. It’s what the Roisins do for each other. Okay?”

I nod. “Tomorrow. Can I go back tomorrow?”

Gran laughs. “I’m so glad you enjoyed your visits. And yes, if you’re ready to go back after school tomorrow, just say the word, and I’ll help you get started again.” She pauses, then closes the scrapbook. “You look exhausted, my dear. Let’s set this aside and get you some dinner and a good night’s sleep, okay?”

I stand up and give her a huge hug, just like the one I gave Roisin the Third a few minutes ago—or, wait—a hundred years ago? I’m definitely not sure how all this works, but as Gran squeezes me tight, I do know one thing. I sure am glad I have the Roisins in my corner.

~~~~~~

I was really dreading day two at this new school, but my visit with the Roisins has kind of taken the edge off. Still, as I settle into my desk across from Diego and watch Olivia and Paige walk in, my heart speeds up just a little. They slide into their seats just as Mr. Garcia writes today's warm-up topic on the whiteboard: B*est Thing You've Done All Week.*

During attendance, Olivia and Paige look at each other and giggle when he says my name. I probably should have expected that. It stings a little, but after meeting the other Roisins yesterday, I like my name a little better now. I'm not sure I'd trade it, even if I could.

"Okay," says Mr. Garcia. "Spend a few minutes on the warmup topic, and then we'll get started with the vocab words for today."

Paige pipes up right away. "This is an easy one. My parents got me a new phone." She holds it up. "And I chose the case. Isn't it the cutest?"

"It looks nice," I tell her—because it actually does. The case is purple and glittery and seems kind of cool.

I'm sitting next to her, and since we usually go in a circle, it's my turn to go next. They all stare at me and wait for my answer.

I'm not sure what to say, so I blurt out the first
~~~~~~

thing that comes to mind. "I looked at a scrapbook with my gran."

Silence. Even from Diego, just for a second. I feel my face turning red. Beet red. Did I just say that out loud? I'd like to explain more, but *I time traveled back to the Irish famine, pioneer days, and a suffragist parade* would probably be worse than what I just said, if that's even possible.

"Cool," says Diego. "Grandmas are the best. I love spending time with mine too."

Olivia and Paige look at each other and laugh. Again. Glad I can provide some entertainment, I guess.

It's Diego's turn to go next, so he starts explaining how he and his brother went to Adventure Zone and played laser tag and mini golf a couple days ago. Apparently, that's one of Olivia's favorite places, too, because the whole table moves on to a new conversation. I make eye contact with Diego and give him a look that says *thank you.* He gives me a quick smile and continues with the story. I relax a little. I'm pretty sure Diego has my back, and now I know the Roisins do too.

I do my best to focus during the rest of the school day, but it's hard not to think about going home and opening the scrapbook. I just wish I didn't have to ride the bus again to get there. Maybe if I sit closer to the front, I can avoid the guys who sat next to me yesterday.

I get to the bus as early as I can and take a seat behind the bus driver, three rows back. The guys from yesterday walk right by me. Crisis averted—at least for today. The bus gets pretty full before a girl from another class asks if anyone is sitting next to me. I say no and move my backpack to the floor. She nods and starts playing a game on her phone.

This might be a chance to meet someone new. I want to introduce myself, but I'm a little scared. What if the words come out wrong? What if she's like Paige and Olivia? What if she gives me a strange look when I say my name?

Then again, what if I make a friend on this bus? What if I have someone to sit next to every day? Maybe I should say hi. Maybe it's worth it. I flash back to something Roisin the First said. *Brave and scared, all at the same time.*

I glance over at the girl's phone and see a covered wagon on her screen. *Is this for real?*

"Cool game," I tell her.

She glances up. "Oh, thanks. It's some retro game my parents got me into called Oregon Trail. It's pretty cool, I guess. Have you played?"

"No, but—." How do I say this? "I've been kind of into history lately."

"You should download it," she says. "We could play two-player."

"Sounds fun." I take out my phone and look the game up on the app store. "I'll try to download it tonight."

She tilts her phone at me to show me her username, *WagonGirlGamer*. "Send me an invitation if you do," she says. "By the way, my real name's Emily."

"I'm Roisin."

She looks up at me again. "Did you say—Roisin?" It comes out a little slow, but I think she's just trying to be careful to say it right.

"Yes. It's Irish. I'm named after my grandmas." I surprise myself a little by how fast that explanation comes. Way easier than it was before I met the Roisins. *Way* easier.

"Cool," she says.

For the rest of the ride, she holds her phone out where I can see it and explains how the game works as she plays it. By the time we get to her stop, I think maybe I've made a friend.

"See you tomorrow?" she asks.

"Sure."

She picks up her backpack and slings it over her back. "I'll save you a seat if I get here first."

"Same," I tell her.

Today's bus ride was so much better than yesterday's. And seriously? *Oregon Trail?* I can't wait to visit more Roisins. I hope Gran lets me get the scrapbook out right away.

At my stop, I hop off the bus and hustle to the front door. Mom's car is still gone. She must be on her way home from the business trip. Gran meets me with fresh cookies again. She usually bakes every day for the first week in a new place. Just another way she's always trying to make things easier for us. I grab a snickerdoodle and give her a kiss on the cheek. "Thanks!" I say. "I have to tell you about what happened on the bus. And also," I look around to make sure the boys can't hear me. "When can I go back to see the Roisins?"

Gran laughs. "Let me get the boys settled," she says. "And I'll meet you in my room at 4:30, okay?"

"Okay." It's only about a half hour away, but it kind of seems like forever. I head up to my room to work on math homework and remind myself to be patient.

At 4:30 on the dot, I stand in front of Gran's room and knock on her door. My breath catches for a second as I notice she's sitting in the rocking chair I saw in Roisin the Second's covered wagon. "You okay?" she asks.

I nod. "Yep. It's just—this chair—I saw it on one of my visits yesterday." Recognition crosses Gran's face. "Ah, yes," she says, rubbing a hand over the smooth wooden arm. "I saw that once, too. How grand." She pauses. "Are you ready?"

"So ready!" I tell her.

I sit down on the bed next to the rocking chair, and we open the book to the page with the Roisin in the old-time Army uniform. Gran squeezes my hand, then lets go. I hold my palm over the page, spread my fingers out wide, take a deep breath, and press my hand to the page. The rush of cold air swirls around me, until I'm not in Gran's room anymore.

Chapter Six:

Roisin the Fourth

1944

"They're five minutes out!"

A gust of wind blows my hair across my face. I push my curls out of the way to try and find out who just said those words. It was a man's voice. He was shouting, and he must have been talking about something pretty important because everyone around me is rushing. Something smells like it's burning. *Where am I?*

I hug the scrapbook close and take in this place like I did the last one—by turning in a slow circle to try and see everything around me. No buildings this time. Just a big, open field with some trees, mountains in the distance, a bunch of people in old-time Army uniforms, and a train sitting on some tracks. I think that's where the burning smell is coming from. The front train car has a chimney sticking out of the top. Way different from the Amtrak we rode to Chicago on family vacation a couple years ago.

I feel someone touch my shoulder and spin around to see a Roisin standing next to me. I know it's her because her red curls are sticking out from under a little brown and white striped hat, and her cheeks are dotted with freckles, just like mine. She's wearing a dress with the same brown and white stripes as the hat. It wraps around with a belt tied in a small bow next to a big pocket on one side.

She makes eye contact with me, then turns and starts walking really fast. We walk past men in soldiers' uniforms and a few women wearing the same outfit as Roisin. I follow her to the other side of the train tracks, behind the train where no one can see us.

She gives me a quick hug, then looks me over. "You must be Roisin the Seventh. I don't believe we've met. I'm Roisin the Fourth. I'm afraid I don't have much time to talk, but it's so very good to see you."

I know how she feels. Hard to explain what a relief it is when I find another Roisin. "Nice to meet you! Where are we?"

"We're in Italy."

Italy. Wow. I want to know everything, all at once. "*When* are we?" I blurt out.

Roisin laughs a little. "Well that's a fitting question, now, isn't it? The year is 1944."

My mind spins. *1944 . . . 1944 . . .* In History last year, we learned the United States was part of World War II from 1941 to 1945.

"Is this—are we in World War II?"

"Yes."

"What are you doing here? I thought only men fought in the war."

"Well, that's kind of true. I'm a nurse. Our part in the fight is to help wounded soldiers recover. Right now, I'm serving on a hospital train. We're taking wounded soldiers to the hospital in Caserta. Some ambulances will be arriving soon, carrying injured soldiers."

Ambulances! No wonder they're all in such a hurry.

She takes me to the space between two train cars and points to a grove of trees on the other side of the tracks. "If you'd like to stay, I'd recommend standing back by those trees as the ambulances come in. Things will move fast, and we're likely to see some pretty bad wounds. It's best to have some training before seeing things like that up close. Plus, even though the others can't see you, you'll probably still feel like you're in the way."

I look her in the eyes and give her one strong

nod. If she needs me to stay by those trees, then that's where I'll be. "Okay. I promise."

"Good. After we get everyone settled, you could hop on the train if you'd like. Prepare yourself, okay? You'll still see some injuries, but things will be less chaotic. How does that sound?"

Overwhelming, I want to say. But there's no time. Ambulances are on their way, and I want to see this Roisin in action. I nod again. She squeezes my hand, points to the trees to remind me where to go, and dashes away.

"Ádh mór ort!" I shout out to her. She doesn't stop running, but she does take a second to turn around and wave to me. Those words mean something to her. They do for me, too—more and more each time I say them.

A rumbling sound fills the air. I'm still standing on the other side of the tracks where Roisin left me, so I peek in between two train cars to see more. At first, I think it's thunder from a storm in the distance, but then I realize it's an engine. A bunch of vehicles are headed this way. They're about the size of ambulances from back home. Instead of being white, though, they're all Army green--the same color as the uniform Dad wears to base every day. They don't have big lights or sirens, but they're coming in fast. Time to go stand by those trees like Roisin told me!

I know the people who work on the hospital train can't see me, but I still make a run for it. Out of instinct, I take a little extra time to race *around* everything instead of straight down the middle. I guess I probably could run right through it all, but that just seems weird.

The scrapbook is tucked tight under one of my arms. I swing the other arm to help me run faster. While I'm running, the ambulances stop. The drivers hop out so fast I wonder if the trucks even finish moving before their combat boots hit the ground.

When I reach the trees, I stop to catch my breath. The ambulances have huge red crosses painted on the side and back. The people from the hospital train pull open the back doors of each ambulance, and everyone gets to work. The wind picks up again. A dark cloud is moving this way. The last thing they need is a thunderstorm while they're trying to get the patients loaded. Thunder rumbles. It doesn't seem to phase anyone, though. They just keep moving.

Some of the ambulances have thin-looking cots with patients on them. The cots have handles on each end that guys in Army uniforms use to lift them out of the ambulance and hand them up to people waiting on the train cars. I hear someone call one of the cots a *stretcher*. Each ambulance must hold four of them because they close the back doors and move on after four patients have been taken out of each one.

One of the soldiers screams as they lift his stretcher out, as if every inch of movement is agonizing for him. My stomach tightens. I've never heard a scream like that before, and I'm pretty sure it's a sound I will never forget. Roisin and another nurse run to his side. Roisin glances down at him and then looks up again. Her body stays put, but she turns her head away to search around her. "I need a doctor. STAT!" she shouts. She grips his hand, looks him in the eyes, and says something I can't hear from where I'm standing. The screaming stops, then changes to a dull groan. I can tell he still hurts, but at least now, he knows someone will take good care of him.

A doctor reaches them, and two people who are already standing in the hospital train help to lift the stretcher on the train. The doctor hops on behind it, and Roisin moves on to her next patient.

Some of the ambulances carry injured soldiers who aren't on stretchers because they can still walk. One soldier with his arm wrapped up uses his other arm to lean on someone for help jumping out of the ambulance. Two soldiers from the hospital train help him over to the train car and lift him up over their shoulders. Three people inside the train reach down to help him in. He cries out like something hurts, bad. "It's okay, soldier. We've got you," the nurse shouts down to him.

One of the soldiers starts to fall as he tries to hop down from the back of the ambulance. The ambulance driver and another injured soldier catch him. The driver looks around. "Lieutenant!" he shouts.

Roisin the Fourth spins around, looks for where the call came from, and starts running. *She's a lieutenant? Amazing.* Then again, she's a Roisin. By now, I shouldn't be surprised.

Roisin grabs an empty stretcher from the ground and drags it behind her to the back of the ambulance where they broke the soldier's fall. After they help the soldier onto the cot, she leans over to take a closer look at him. He doesn't seem to be awake, but she still says something to him before nodding the okay to lift him into the train.

Finally, the ambulances are empty. It's a good thing because the thunder sounds are getting closer, and a streak of lightning just shot through the sky. I remember what Roisin said about hopping on the train, and I take off running with the scrapbook again, this time straight through the field instead of around it. I am not missing this. One huge raindrop splashes on my neck just as I hop up into one of the cars. Seconds later, a downpour of rain hits the roof and echoes through the train. I'm so glad the injured soldiers are safe inside now.

The train makes a loud sound I haven't heard before, kind of half-way between a huff and a hiss. White steam rolls by outside the window and mixes with the rain. The car I'm on has rows of bunk beds on each side with a passageway in the middle. The bunks are stacked two high, and they're full of injured soldiers. I'm not sure what to do. I wish I could help somehow, but that's not how this works. I remind myself only Roisin can see me. And here she comes, walking straight at me.

She grabs my hand without looking at it and pulls me along behind her—through another train car full of beds, across a platform, and into a car with some tables and chairs. For now, we're the only two in this one.

"It's a lot to take in," she says. "How are you?"

"Fine." I pause to look at her. "You are amazing."

"I'm only doing what I was trained to. But I must get back to it. Things will be a little busy while we get everyone settled in, and you do look a bit tired. You could rest here for a while if you'd like."

"I wish I could help."

"That would be grand, but we both know that's not an option. Besides, you've been a big help to me already, just by visiting. You remind me there is a world and a future outside this war. I *will* get through this."

"Nurse!" A man yells for help from the car next door.

"I must go," says Roisin. "Please, rest a bit, and then come and find me."

I nod to her and watch as she dashes across the platform and back into one of the cars with the bunks. Part of me wants to hop up to follow her and watch her in action, but instead, I do what I've been told and settle into one of the seats in the dining car. The chug of the engine is constant. It has a rhythm to it, almost like a song or a lullaby. I lean my head back against the window and feel sleep overtake me.

~~~~~

"Oof. It sure feels good to finally sit down."

My eyes shoot open as I hear someone talking at a table beside me. I gasp and stand up before I remember where I am and remind myself no one else can see me.

The person who talked must be a nurse because she has the same uniform as Roisin. She's sitting across from a soldier. They're both drinking coffee and eating food from tin trays. It smells good.

Wait! My hands are empty! My heart thumps, and a knot forms in my stomach. Where is the scrapbook? I find it on the seat next to where I was sitting, scoop it up, and hold it tight. *How long was I out,* I wonder. Blue skies and puffy clouds have replaced the rain outside. Time to go find Roisin.

The train shifts back and forth a little as it moves, so I have to lean against the wall every once in a while to keep my balance. I walk through the dining car, across the platform, and into one of the cars with patients in it.

Next to me, one of the soldiers has his arm raised in a splint, but he's using the other arm to hold up a copy of a newspaper called *Stars and Stripes.*
~~~~~

On the bunk below him, a guy with a stethoscope is listening to the heart of a sleeping patient. Maybe that's one of the doctors. He seems satisfied with what he heard because he stands up, nods to a nurse, and walks down a few beds to check on a different patient.

One bed down, a soldier in one of the bunks is leaning against the wall behind him, sitting up just a little. I watch a nurse feed him a piece of bread. His arms are stretched out on top of the blanket that covers him. The arms look bruised, and both hands are wrapped in white gauze. No wonder the nurse is feeding him. There's no way he could feed himself right now. It makes me wonder what happened to him out there. Will his hands be okay? I imagine how scared I would feel if I were hurt and far away from home. I'm glad people like Roisin are here to help take care of him.

He finishes chewing. "Would you like some more coffee?" asks his nurse.

"Yes ma'am," says the soldier.

The nurse pulls something from her tray that looks like a cross between a coffee cup and a teapot. It's small like a coffee mug, but it has a handle and a spout. The nurse tips the mug up, and the soldier drinks from the spout. He swallows, and a smile sprawls across his face.

"Hits the spot," he says. "Thank you."

"You're most welcome," says the nurse. She

pats him on the shoulder. "Can I get you anything else, Sargeant?"

He shakes his head no. She nods. "Very well. I'll be back to check on you in a bit." She moves on to the next patient.

Since Roisin isn't in this car, I decide to move on too. I cross another platform between the cars and find Roisin at the far end of the next one, sitting beside another soldier. She smiles at me as I walk in. I kneel on one knee on the floor next to her chair. She has a bowl of soup in her lap. "Do you think you could take one more bite?" she asks him.

He shakes his head yes, so she scoops up a spoonful and carefully slides it into his mouth. He swallows, then holds his hand up to signal he's had enough.

"Very good, soldier!" she tells him. "You'll have your strength back before you know it."

He looks so tired. By the time Roisin puts the bowl of soup down on the tray, he's already closed his eyes and doesn't open them again when she helps him lay back from his sitting position. "Rest easy," she whispers.

I follow her as she carries the half-filled bowl to another car, empties the leftovers into a trash can, and sets the bowl next to some other dirty dishes. She pulls a small round watch from the pocket of her nurse's uniform. "We should be arriving at the division hospital soon," she says. "We'll help unload the patients and then move on to our next pickup site."

Wow. "But, will you have a chance to rest first?" I ask.

"Probably," she answers. She sits down and lets out a sigh. "It just depends on when they need us next."

I try to find the right words to let her know what I think of her work, but all that comes out is "This is . . . you are . . . *Wow.*"

Roisin laughs a little. "Thank you. It's an honor to help these soldiers." She lets out a small yawn. I can only imagine how tired she must be.

I'd love to stay and ask more questions, but I want to give her time to rest before the train arrives at the hospital. Plus, we're alone in this car now, but it's only a matter of time before someone else joins us. I look down at the scrapbook. "I guess it's time for me to move on," I say.

"Well, then," says Roisin. "I surely did enjoy your visit. Thank you for reminding me of the world outside this war. I needed that. Very much, in fact."

I reach out to hug her. "Thank *you,*" I say. "I've learned so much." I look her in the eyes one more time to thank her before I open the scrapbook. This next Roisin is standing next to a space shuttle. *A space shuttle!*

I'm so excited about this next one I almost forget to feel scared. *Almost.* I take a deep breath, hold my palm over the page, and press down. The cool breeze starts swirling around me—until I am not on the hospital train anymore.

Chapter Seven:

Roisin the Fifth

1983

Whoosh.

I hear something zip by me and realize that for the first time, I'm sitting when I land instead of standing. The scrapbook is in my lap, and wind is blowing its pages open. It's also dark, but I do see flashes of bright lights every few seconds. Wait. Am I . . . moving?

"Oh dear!" says someone sitting next to me. "What a grand surprise. Let me find a place to pull over, and we can get things situated."

Pull over? Oh, that makes sense! It dawns on me I must be in a car with the windows rolled down. The car slows. I brush the hair out of my face and look over at the person sitting beside me. Yep, she's a Roisin! And this one looks extra familiar. It's something about the eyes, like maybe I've seen them before.

Then, it hits me. Goosebumps run up and down my arms.

Gran?

I guess I was expecting this, but I'm not sure I was ready for it.

She pulls the car over to the side of the road, eyes the scrapbook in my lap, and looks me over. "Well, hello!" she says. "I don't believe we've met yet. I'm Roisin the Fifth. And you must be Roisin the Seventh." Seriously? How do the Roisins figure that out so fast every single time? "What a pleasure it is to meet you," she says.

Meet me? I mean, we've already met. But I guess technically, she wouldn't remember since I haven't even been born yet. My thoughts start spinning so fast it feels like they might burst right out through my ears. I take a deep breath and decide just to go with it. I'm not missing out on this chance to learn more about Gran.

"Good to . . . see you," I say. The word *meet* just doesn't seem exactly right.

She looks at her watch. "We don't have much time, so we better get going. I'll explain on the way. See that handle on your door?"

I look over at my door and point to a metal

thing that looks a little like a lever. "This one?"

"Yes. If you spin it, your window will roll up, and you won't have all the wind blowing hair in your face."

I try spinning the handle. It does exactly what Gran said it would. I guess cars were a little different during Gran's time.

"Perfect!" she says. "Now, let's get going."

I reach up to buckle my seatbelt, and before I know it, we're on our way again. "Where are we?" I ask.

"We just passed through Jacksonville, Florida," she says. "We're on our way to Cape Canaveral to watch the Space Shuttle launch. I thought I would be watching alone. What a treat to have a Roisin along to enjoy it with me!"

The Space Shuttle? Gran has talked about the space program a few times, but I didn't know it meant this much to her. "Okay," I say. By now, I know the next question to ask. "*When* are we?"

"Today is June 18, 1983. Has been for about four hours now. I'm coming from Fort Dix, New Jersey, where my husband—." She pauses and shakes her head a little. "I guess maybe I should say, *your grandfather,* is stationed in the Army." I guess this whole granddaughter thing might be a lot for her to take in, too. "I stopped at a hotel last night and got up extra early this morning to be sure to make it on time."

"On time?"

"Yes. For the launch."

I look out my window. It's still dark. Stars fill the sky. "I guess I didn't know you were this interested in the space program."

"Well, I am, but today's launch is extra special. NASA is sending the first American woman into space. Her name is Sally Ride."

Sally Ride. I remember reading an article about her in Science class a couple years ago. And I think her name is in a song Gran used to play when we were little. "I know that name," I tell her.

"Well, I should hope so!" says Gran. "Did you know she was one of 8,000 people who applied for the space program? Six women and twenty-nine men were chosen, and Sally was the only woman who made it all the way to the space shuttle crew. I think she's amazing!"

Sure sounds like it. I mean, you'd have to be pretty amazing to become one in 8,000.

"She has a PhD in Physics from Stanford," Gran tells me. "And if you watch her in TV interviews, she just seems to have it all together. Smart. Humble. If you can't tell, I'm a big fan. History will be made today, and we're going to watch it happen."

This is a different side of Gran. I'm not sure I've ever seen her quite this excited.

Her eyes move to the instrument panel on her

car, and her smile turns into a small frown. "My gas tank is a little low. I guess we're going to have to stop." A few minutes later, I hear the click-click-click of her blinker as she pulls into the gas station.

Gran parks the car and puts the hose in to fill the tank. Then, she pops the hood on the front. Oh no! My family only does that when something isn't right. What happened? I step out.

"What's wrong?" I ask.

"Nothing, I hope," she says. "I just need to check the oil."

A guy from the gas station came out. "Can I help you, ma'am?" he asks.

"Thanks," says Gran, "but I think I have it under control."

The man looks a little surprised. I'm not. That's just Gran for you. "If you say so," he says, raising an eyebrow. "I'll be inside when you need me."

Gran waves a quick thank you to him and gets to work. She uses a paper towel from the gas station to check the oil level on a stick from under the hood. "A little low," she says, before grabbing a container from the trunk, opening up another part under the hood, and pouring the liquid from the container into it. Then, she uses the stick to check it one more time. It must look okay because she puts the lid back on the place where she poured the oil and then closes the hood. "Should be all set now," she says, just before looking at her watch again. "We better get going!"

The rest of the drive goes pretty quickly. Gran tells me a little more about Sally Ride and the other astronauts on the shuttle mission. When we see a sign for Cape Canaveral, a giant smile sprawls across her face. The sun is just starting to rise. We're moving along great until traffic starts to slow down, big time. Gran definitely isn't the only one interested in watching this launch. Our car has been stopped in traffic for about half an hour when she makes a decision. "I'm going to pull over at the next parking spot we can find, and then we'll walk to a spot where we can watch the launch. How does that sound?"

"Sounds good!" I tell her, secretly wondering if we'll even make it on time. But with the looks of this traffic, walking seems like the only option that just might work.

Gran pulls over into a big field where someone is collecting three dollars to let people park there. She hands over the money, and we both climb out of the car. I slide over to scoot out from her side, so it won't look like an invisible person is opening the passenger door.

Gran points to some trees in the distance. "I bet we can see the launch from there," she tells me. Her eyes sparkle with anticipation. "Let's go!"

The closer we get, the bigger the crowds grow. Grandparents with their grandkids, high school kids who look like they might be on a date, moms and daughters, and whole families are out here ready to watch. A few people are wearing t-shirts with the words *Ride, Sally, Ride* on them. Gran tells me those are lyrics from a song written almost twenty years ago. A few blocks later, we hear music, and Gran says the song they're playing is the one from the t-shirts.

My mouth falls open, and I feel my eyes get big as I realize why I know this song. It's called "Mustang Sally," and when my brothers and I were little, Gran used to play it in the living room so we could dance to it and get our energy out on days when it was too cold or rainy to play outside. I shake off my surprise and stop myself from the urge to start dancing right here and now. It happens every time I hear this song. And now that I know why Gran liked it so much, it makes me love the song even more. I never thought much about Gran's life before she was . . . well . . . *Gran.* Amazing. All of it.

We walk a while longer until there are so many people we can't move up anymore. Gran stops and gives me a playful nudge. I want to hug her, but since no one can see me, all that will do is make her look like she's hugging air. Instead, I look at her with a smile and say, "I guess this is our spot."

She gives me another giant grin like the one I've seen from her my whole life when she's excited about something. I love that grin and the way it always makes me feel like everything is right in the world. Then, just like everyone else, we wait.

I look around and notice a big group of TV cameras way ahead of us. In the distance, across some water and behind a bunch of trees, I squint to see a platform with a metal tower next to it on one side and the space shuttle on the other. Everything becomes a little clearer as the sun rises higher and brings a little light with it.

Suddenly, we hear something rumble. Gran perks up and straightens her back. "I think this might be it!" she says.

Gran and I both stand on our tiptoes to see just a little better. The rumbling continues. Suddenly, the crowd starts counting down from ten. In the distance, big puffs of white and gray smoke shoot out from beside the shuttle. Four, three, two, one . . . I know they can't hear me, but I can't help shouting the numbers out along with everyone else. I want to be part of this.

The puffs of smoke get bigger, like there's a huge cloud on the ground racing to get to its place in the sky. A lady next to me yells "Yes" and pumps her fist, and a little boy next to her starts jumping up and down like my brother Aidan always does on Christmas morning.

The shuttle is attached to one huge-looking rocket, with two smaller rockets on the side. The kid standing next to me who was just jumping up and down tugs at the sleeve of the lady who is with him. "Will those rockets stay on the whole time?" he asks.

The lady next to him ruffles his hair. "Nope," she says. "They'll detach. They're just giving the shuttle enough power to make it into space."

I hear people around me chanting "Ride, Sally Ride!" Gran joins them, and even though Gran is the only one who can hear me, I add my voice to the mix. We watch as the shuttle rises higher and higher. Bright fire shoots from the bottom of the rockets, followed by puffy white smoke and some dark smoke at the bottom, until the shuttle is out of sight.

People start clapping and hugging each other. I look up at Gran. She shakes her head a little, like she's too amazed at what happened to say anything. Her eyes are a little wet. I move closer to her and hug the scrapbook close.

Gran looks up at the sky. "Ádh mór ort," she whispers.

"Ádh mór ort," I add.

After a few minutes, Gran takes a deep breath. "Well," she says, "Time to head home!"

It takes us a while to get back to the car because there are so many people here, and we can't really talk much because it will look like Gran is talking to herself. It's okay with me, though. Just walking beside her and being part of this day is more than good enough.

Finally, we reach the car. She opens the door on the driver's side and waits for a second as I sit down and slide over to the other side. I'm really starting to understand the rules of this Roisin visit thing. I'm getting pretty good at it, too—even if I do say so myself.

Once we're in the car, Gran reaches over and grips my hand. "I'm so happy I could share this with a Roisin," she says.

I squeeze her hand tighter. Then, I look over and try to store all the things about younger Gran in my memory. Red frizzy hair, just like mine. Smooth skin, without many wrinkles—except for those trademark smile lines on the sides of her mouth. Those same sparkly eyes. And even if she won't remember what we said to each other today, I feel super lucky *this* Roisin will still be part of my life when I go back home.

I open the scrapbook and turn to the last page. It's the photo of me.

"Ready to move on?" asks Gran.

"Yes, I think I am."

"What a joy it was to meet you, Roisin the Seventh. And I guess I'll be seeing you again someday."

"Just so you know, you're going to be an amazing grandma."

"I imagine you make it easy," she says.

I look around to make sure no one is standing around to see us before reaching over to give her a "goodbye for now" hug. Then, I stretch out my hand and hold it over the open page. I take a deep breath and press my hand on the photo. The swirling air surrounds me, until I'm not in Gran's car anymore.

98

Chapter Eight

Present Day

I'm right back where I started, sitting on the bed in Gran's room with the scrapbook in my lap. Gran stands up from the rocking chair and sits next to me on the bed. She reaches her arm around my shoulder and gives me a squeeze. "Welcome back," she says.

"I was just with you!" I say. "We saw the space shuttle launch. With Sally Ride!"

Gran smiles. "It was such a treat to share that day with you."

"You remember?"

"Well, I know you were there. I don't know anything we talked about because that's the way this works. Remember—knowing the future could change the present, and we can't have that now, can we? But I do remember we shared those moments together. And that's the most important part."

"How come Mom wasn't in the book? She's a Roisin! Does she make visits too?"

"Oh, yes. Your mother has her own scrapbook, just like all the Roisins do. But we can only visit our grandmothers. That's why your mom's story isn't in your book."

Suddenly, a new thought hits me. "Wait! Will Roisins come to visit me now too?"

"They sure will," says Gran. "You'll even know which Roisin is which. It will just come to you when you see them. None of us are quite sure why it works that way, but it does. Every single time."

I hear the garage door open. Does that mean Mom is home? Gran and I talk a little longer, and I hear a knock on her door. "Come in," says Gran.

"There you are," says Mom. "What are you two—" Mom sees the Book of Roisins on my lap and stops, mid-sentence. She steps all the way inside Gran's room and closes the door behind her. Then, she stands a little taller, tilts her head to the side, and gives Gran one of those smiles you give when you're sure the other person knows exactly what you're thinking.

"Did you . . . make some visits?" asks Mom. Tears brim in her eyes. She moves closer to us.

I stand up and give her a hug. "Yes," I whisper. "It was amazing."

Mom pulls back and takes my hands. "I know it can be hard to be the youngest. Especially when you have four big brothers. But I hope meeting the Roisins helped you understand how long I waited and hoped for you. And how important you are. To all of us."

Before I can say anything, I hear the boys tromping down the hall outside Gran's door. One of them knocks, and Gran tells them to come in.

Joe's carrying a basketball. "I won!" he proclaims.

"Only because you cheated," says Aidan.

"What's for dinner?" asks Patrick.

"Homemade pizza," says Mom. "Now wash up, boys. You're going to help me make it."

The boys head to the kitchen, and Mom starts to follow.

"Mom?" I call out to her.

"Yes?"

"I'm glad I'm a Roisin."

~~~~~

I stand at the mirror and adjust my headband until it's exactly the way I like it. The notecards in my hand are shaking a little. Today is kind of a big day. I look down at my notes.

"Hello," I practice. "My name is Roisin. I moved to—"

"Roisin! Breakfast!" Mom's words float up from the kitchen and make me look over at the clock.
~~~~~

How did it get to be 7:30 already? Ready or not, I guess it's time to go.

The smell of bacon and eggs wafts up the stairs. Gran must have woken up extra early to make them for me. I mean, I guess she made them for everyone, really, but today she made them *because* of me. Today is Westview Middle School's monthly assembly. Which means it's my turn to introduce myself to the school.

I shove my notecards in my pocket, give myself a nod in the mirror, and head downstairs to breakfast. Mom's standing at the counter with her hands wrapped around a mug of coffee. "Morning!" she says.

Dad's usually gone by now, but today he's sitting at the table in his everyday fatigues, lacing up his combat boots. "There she is!" he says. "Couldn't leave today without wishing you a little luck." He walks over to me and gives me a squeeze from the side. "You've got this, Roshie. You'll do great." I love the way he uses a shorter version of my name sometimes. And now, I love the longer version, too.

"Thanks, Pops," I tell him. He walks over to Mom, kisses her on the cheek, waves to Gran and the boys, and heads out the door.

Gran taps the seat next to her at the table. There's a plate, complete with scrambled eggs just the way I like them and two pieces of bacon made my favorite way—extra crispy. There's also a pile of mixed fruit on the side. "We saved you a spot," she says.

I feel like Irish dancers are doing a jig in my stomach, but the food looks so good I still eat every bit. I wash it down with some water and a quick swig of orange juice.

"Okay. I think I'm ready."

"I *know* you're ready," says Gran.

Joe's at the stove grabbing another piece of bacon. "Hey, Roisin!" he says. "Thanks for having to give a speech or whatever. If it makes Gran make bacon for breakfast, I'm all for it. Good luck!"

"Thanks."

Patrick is putting some eggs on a piece of toast. Aidan and Joe are standing by the front door waiting to leave for school. They're having a loud debate about how many people it would take to stop a charging rhinoceros. I could weigh in, but right now, I have other things on my mind.

I pick up my plate, rinse it, and add it to the pile the boys have already started. Then, I grab my backpack from its hook and decide to go out through the garage to avoid getting caught up in the rhinoceros debate.

I pass Mom and Gran. "Thanks for breakfast and for saving me some bacon," I say.

On the way out, I turn to glance at them behind me. Mom gives me one of her *you've got this* nods. Gran waves.

I know what's coming next.

"Ádh mór ort" blends together in both of their voices. This time, the words weave through the kitchen and wrap around me like a warm blanket at one of Joe's late season football games. I smile at them and close the door behind me.

~~~~~

Paige and Olivia are already in their seats by the time I get to the classroom. As usual, they keep talking like I'm not even there—which is way better than the "poodle hair" comment from the first day, I've decided. I put my math notebook in my desk and set out the English homework Mr. Garcia will collect this morning. My hand moves down to my pocket, just to make sure the notecards for my assembly speech are still there. It's empty! My heart thumps like Aidan practicing his drums until I remember I have another pocket and realize my notes are tucked safely in it.

Phew. That was close. Thankfully, Paige and Olivia are too busy talking to even notice. In fact, I think they might even be . . . arguing?

Diego slides into his desk chair just as the bell rings. He gives me a quick wave.

"Good morning, everyone!" says Mr. Garcia. "We don't have much time for homeroom this morning because of the assembly, but I'd like to
~~~~~

collect your English homework. Please set it on your desk, and I'll be coming around the room in a minute. I'll be going over the requirements for your next journal entry while I collect them, so please listen carefully and take notes if you need to."

Diego unzips his backpack and shuffles through papers. "I know I did it!" he mumbles to himself. "I finished it yesterday."

I know he did it too because I watched him slide it into a folder before he left. That's not the folder he's looking in now, though. I nudge him until he looks up at me. We're not supposed to be talking, so I mouth *purple folder* as clearly as I can at him.

Diego's face lights up, and I can tell he remembers. He grabs his purple folder and pulls his homework out just in time to set it out before Mr. Garcia gets there. *Thank you,* he mouths back to me. We definitely have each other's backs like that. It's one thing I've learned in my three weeks at this new school.

"Oh my gosh. Would you just shut up about the stupid flute? You'll do *fine!*" Olivia's whisper-yell to Paige carries so far across the room even Mr. Garcia turns to look at them. I don't think she meant for it to be so loud because her face turns about as red as one of Gran's roses, and Paige looks down at her notebook and makes her shoulders small, like she wishes she could just sink into the floor and not come out until the classroom is empty. Boy, do I know that feeling.

Three short beeps sound over the intercom, and our principal's voice fills the classroom. "Good morning, Westview Wombats!" she says. "As most of you know, we'll be starting today with an assembly. Three new students will be introducing themselves, and four of our band students will be performing solos for us. We'll also be cheering on our sixth-grade boys' basketball team before their game tonight. Teachers, please bring your students to the gym."

Mr. Garcia moves over to the classroom door. "This morning, we are fortunate enough to have *two* classmates presenting at the assembly. Roisin will be introducing herself, and Paige will be sharing a flute solo with us. Be sure to cheer them on! Now, let's go."

Olivia stands up right away and starts walking. Paige stays in her chair.

"Are you coming?" asks Olivia.

"In a minute." Paige's voice is quiet.

"Fine."

Diego stands up and waits for me. I glance at Paige. "I'll catch up," I tell him.

I think back to Roisin the Second and how happy she was to see me when she was on the frontier. Then, I think of how excited Gran was for Sally Ride, and all the other people that day who were excited for her too. Things sure are better when we support each other.

Maybe Paige has never had a chance to see that.

Maybe it's my turn to show her.

Almost the whole class is lined up by the door. Paige grabs her flute from beside her desk and stands up too.

"Paige?" I say.

She looks up at me. "Yeah?"

"I heard you practicing in band yesterday. You sounded really good. Don't worry. I think you'll do great."

Paige looks a little surprised. She stares down at her shoes, then looks back up at me. "Thanks."

"Good luck," I tell her.

"You too."

We don't say anything else as Paige and I walk behind Diego all the way to the gym.

~~~~~

I wish they had some fans or something in here. The gym feels stuffy as Mrs. Bittelberg welcomes everyone and goes over the plan for the assembly. First up? New student introductions, of course. The Irish dancers are back in my stomach, and my heart is pounding so hard I can feel it in my ears again. I reach down again to make sure those notecards are still in my pocket. *You're a Roisin,* I remind myself. *You've got this.*
~~~~~

Mrs. Bittelberg announces my name. My legs feel like jelly as I walk to the podium. My mouth already feels like it's filled with sand. I pull my notecards out of my pocket, plop them on the podium, and look up.

That's when I see them, standing in the back of the gym.

The Roisins are here.

From Roisin the First all the way to Gran and Mom, they're standing together, holding hands and giving me that *you've got this* look. Gran and Mom look normal, but everyone else looks faded, like I can see through them a little. They're definitely here, though. Every single one of them.

Whoa. I have no idea how this part works. I for sure have to ask Mom and Gran about this later. For now, though, I won't question it. I'll just soak it in.

I clear my throat and look down at my notecards.

"Hello," I say, a little surprised by how loud and clear my voice sounds in the microphone. "My name is Roisin."

Author Bio:

Tracy Schuldt Helixon began her writing career at age five, when her parents found her writing all over her little brother. When they asked what she was doing, she said, "Timmy thought he was a piece of paper." To Timmy's relief, Tracy now uses a computer to write. Today, Tracy is an award-winning author and passionate teacher who chases creativity, kindness, faith, coffee, and chocolate.

Social Media:
Facebook: Tracy Schuldt Helixon, Author
Twitter: @THelixon
Website: https://tracyhelixon.com/
Pinterest: Tracy Schuldt Helixon, Author
Goodreads: Tracy Schuldt Helixon
Instagram: tracy_schuldt_helixon_author
Bluesky: @tracy-s-helixon.bsky.social

Published Books:

Fields of Promise Series: https://amzn.to/4jOlawS
Sweet Surprises: https://amzn.to/43EU6eN

Little Isaac's Big Adventure:
https://amzn.to/43Qk2o1
Walter's Light: https://amzn.to/43Qk2o1

www.ingramcontent.com/pod-product-compliance
Lightning Source LLC
Chambersburg PA
CBHW060504300726
48975CB00008B/2639